C IS FOR COEDS

Also by Alison Tyler

———

Best Bondage Erotica

Best Bondage Erotica 2

Exposed

Got a Minute?

The Happy Birthday Book of Erotica

Heat Wave: Sizzling Sex Stories

Luscious: Stories of Anal Eroticism

The Merry XXXmas Book of Erotica

Red Hot Erotica

Slave to Love

Three-Way

Caught Looking (with Rachel Kramer Bussel)

A Is for Amour

B Is for Bondage

D Is for Dress-Up

C IS FOR COEDS

EROTIC STORIES
EDITED BY ALISON TYLER

CLEIS
PRESS

Published in the United States by Cleis Press Inc.,
P.O. Box 14697, San Francisco, California 94114.

Printed in the United States.
Cover design: Scott Idleman
Text design: Karen Quigg
Cleis Press logo art: Juana Alicia
First Edition.
10 9 8 7 6 5 4 3 2 1

ACKNOWLEDGMENTS

Cheerful Commendations go to:

Adam Nevill

Barbara Pizio

Felice Newman

Frédérique Delacoste

Diane Levinson

Violet Blue

and SAM, always.

Personally, I am always ready to learn, although I do not always like being taught. —WINSTON CHURCHILL

CONTENTS

INTRODUCTION:
EXTRACURRICULAR ACTIVITIES

CLOSE YOUR EYES.

Breathe in deep.

Can you smell that?

Fallen leaves stirred by crisp breezes. Autumn is in the air. Back-to-school sales are featured in every shiny newspaper pull-out. And I'm flashing back to my days at UCLA. I was a vague, daydreaming sort of student, focused far more on my off-campus jobs—working on newspapers and for indie magazines and on a radio station—than on my homework.

Yet I loved the atmosphere of the school. Loved being able to say I was a *college coed.* Oh, what a thrill, what a perfect description. The words rolled off my tongue at parties. And the men's eyes always lit up.

There is something so damn sexy about the pulse that beats on campuses. If I could have simply skipped the lectures—why on earth did I take Christian Iconography or Ancient Chinese Artifacts?—and basked in the hot sun at the sculpture garden, eavesdropped all day in the campus coffeehouses, and fucked against the outdoor balconies in my dorm house, without the guilt that plagued me, I would have scored an A+ in every single one of my outrageous extracurricular activities.

I probably would also have been able to pay more attention in class had I taken courses called "Cunnilingus 101" (a slippery sex story by the divine Rachel Kramer Bussel) or "Janelle's Spankology 101" (Michelle Houston's thrilling spanking three-way). I'd have creamed to be over the lap of the professor in Greta Christina's "This Week," and even if I never attend a "College Reunion," I can fantasize about visiting one like Andrea Dale's.

What makes college tales so ferociously erotic? Colleges are places not just of intellectual awakening, but also erotic awakening—like in "Sugar" by Brooke Stern and "While She Was Dancing" by Thomas S. Roche. And coeds appeal not only to each other, but also to their elders—as witness the seductive "Call Me Jenny" by the ever-sultry Savannah Stephens Smith.

Whether you're heading back to school, or recalling the gold-drenched days of your own university adventures, *C Is for Coeds* should undoubtedly be at the top of your required reading list.

XXX,
Alison Tyler

BROOKE STERN

SUGAR

C ALL ME CRAZY, but after I heard from Ted that Megan wanted to be spanked, she was the only thing I could think about that whole semester.

She didn't live in our dorms. She lived in the girls' dorms across campus, that promised land where we freshmen never set foot. I never found out how Ted met Megan. She just appeared one day, riding shotgun in his car and wearing all black. She popped cassettes that we'd never heard before in and out of the stereo as we drove. I would have been too scared to go out with someone from a tribe so different from our own, but Ted wasn't. Because she was with him, we accepted her, like we accepted it when he told us where we were going or what we were doing. Besides, it's not as if the rest of us were bringing many girls around that semester.

Anyway, a few days after we met her, Ted dropped the bombshell. We were drinking beer and playing Nintendo in Scott's dorm room, and Ted said, "Remember Megan? Well, she sucked my dick and asked me if I'd spank her." Scott asked if he was bullshitting and he said no. I was dying to ask whether he did it or not, but I didn't want to seem too interested. Then Ted answered my question without my even having to ask. "I'm not into sick shit like that," he said, and we all hooted and told him to shut up and threw Scott's dirty clothes at him. Ted was exactly the guy who *was* into sick shit like that. He claimed to have fucked a senior Kappa girl up the ass. We all knew he was most likely lying, but still we jacked off to the thought of it. We didn't hassle him about stories like that because otherwise we might have gotten hassled about our own stories. Most of us were still virgins, but we had been lying about it since prom, and it was as if we had some secret agreement to accept each other's stories without asking too many questions.

Even after six beers, I could hardly sleep that night for thinking about Megan. I got up as if to piss, but I walked to the bathroom at the other end of the hall so no one would walk in while I was jerking off. Afterward, though, I thought it was a pretty stupid thing to want to do, and Ted was probably lying anyway.

Megan wasn't in Ted's car next time he came around, and we didn't ask what had happened. Even after a few weeks passed and Ted began to regale us with stories of some other conquest, Megan was the one I remembered. Maybe the other guys stopped thinking about her, but I didn't. Well, I should say that I didn't stop thinking about spanking—a lifelong interest that I didn't dare tell anyone about—and she was the first real girl I'd ever had to put a face on my fantasies. After a while, though, she became as distant from reality as my elaborate masturbatory fantasies of bare bottoms raised to meet stinging slaps or white cotton panties red with blood from a wicked caning.

Toward the end of the semester, we were required to go and hear some motivational speaker out at the college's retreat center. After a while, I had had enough and was wandering slowly in the direction of the portajohns when I heard someone say hi to me. I'd been looking down, kicking a nut or something, and when I looked up, I saw Megan standing just a few feet in front of me.

"Pretty lame, huh?" she asked.

"Yeah."

"Ted here?"

"Yeah."

"Well?"

"Yeah."

It got silent and I didn't want her to go, but I couldn't think of anything to say that wasn't stupid. It was beyond me to be clever or witty; it took all my concentration just to keep from looking at her ass.

"Want to go for a walk?" she finally asked. Thank God.

"Yeah."

We walked silently while I wished I had said something other than "yeah" three times. She kicked the nut I had been kicking and then I kicked it again. I dug my hands in my pockets and was glad when our elbows accidentally touched.

"What do you want to talk about?" she asked.

"I don't know."

"Jeez, Brian. Say something."

"Something."

She started to laugh.

"Now I can see why Ted said you never get laid."

Shit. If I had been tongue-tied before, it was twice as bad now. She turned and faced me, upping an ante that was already too rich for a coward like me.

"Tell me what you like, Brian."

She was so beautiful it was scary. I said the first thing I saw.

"I like your eyes."

"That's so stupid. I mean, what do you like to do?"

"When?"

"When do *you* think?"

"I like to go down on girls."

I thought that sounded gutsy. Even though I'd never done it, girls were supposed to love it.

"That's better."

We started walking again.

"Know what I like?"

"No."

"Ted didn't tell you?"

"No."

"I like to be spanked."

"Have you ever been spanked?"

"Have you ever gone down on a girl?"

"No."

"Me neither."

"Gone down on a girl?"

"No, idiot. Been spanked."

"Can I kiss you?"

"Yeah."

We started kissing. As soon as I thought it would be okay, I grabbed her ass, kneading the flesh and hoping she would know how badly I wanted to spank her. Then she stopped kissing me.

"Don't just feel my ass. Tell me what you want to do to it."

"I want to spank it."

"And?"

"I want to pull down your panties and spank it."

"Go on."

"I want to make you pull down your panties and make you lie over my lap and spank you ten times, as hard as I can."

"That's better."

We both laughed, not sure if we were serious. I went to kiss her again but she backed away.

"I dare you."

"What?"

"Are you slow or something?"

"Here?"

"You're the boss. You tell me."

We weren't too deep into the woods. It was getting dark, but we could still hear the motivational speaker over the P.A. system and the crowd clapping. My friends would have expected me back ten minutes ago.

"Pull down your pants."

So help me, she did.

"And your panties."

It was the first time I'd even seen it.

I sat down on a fallen tree and told her to lie across my lap.

It was impossibly awkward, but she managed it anyway. I raised my hand above my head and spanked her once. It wasn't hard, not nearly as hard as I could, but still I spanked her. It was loud and I was terrified someone might hear. She let out a giggle. It was probably because she was nervous, but I worried she was laughing at me, so I spanked her again, harder this time because she had giggled. I alternated cheeks—oh, miraculous cheeks—with each spank, watching my red handprints appear, confirming that I was actually doing it. My head was throbbing, and if it had been possible for a nineteen-year-old to burst a blood vessel and have a stroke, I would have. I literally felt light-headed by the time we got to ten, and I had no idea what to do next. Luckily, she just slid down to her knees between my legs, undid my pants, and began sucking my cock. It wasn't hard and I thought she would think the worst of me, but she was unfazed and took no time at all to become the first girl to ever make me come.

My hands tingled and my knees felt weak when I stood up. I was still brushing dirt and bits of bark off my pants and trying to coax my hard on down when I slid into the seat next to Ted.

"There was a line," I whispered to him. He rolled his eyes.

When I called her, I was afraid it would be awkward and we wouldn't be able to talk about it. I shouldn't have worried.

"How are you?" I asked

"My butt's a little sore. How are you?"

Oh, my God.

"Fine."

"You don't say much, do you, Brian?"

"I guess not."

"That's okay. I still like you."

That was exactly the sort of thing that usually tripped me up, but this time I got it right.

"I like you too, Megan."

"I bet you say that to all the girls you spank."

"Whatever."

She wasn't the only one who could be snide.

"You want to come over?"

"Is your roommate there?"

"Of course not."

"You want me to bring some beer?" I asked, trying to make up for being lame.

"Is beer all guys can think about?"

"No."

All I could think about was spanking her, but I was too scared to say it.

"Then get over here and we'll try to come up with something better to do than get drunk."

It was just after school, and light poured in through her window. In the light of day, it was even scarier. Even she didn't have anything smart to say, so we just started kissing. Then we stopped and I knew what to do. I sat down and she began to unbuckle her belt but then she mumbled something that might have been "Wait a minute," and started rummaging through her dresser. A catalog of everything that I could possibly have done wrong passed through my head before she turned around and walked back to me.

"Use this," she said, her voice soft, cracking.

She handed me a paddle, lacquered pine, about eight inches long and a third of an inch thick. I took it by the handle and it was heavier than I thought it would be.

She pulled her jeans and panties down to the crook of her knees and lay across my lap. She stretched her arms out on the couch, gripping the end of the cushion as if she had done this before. I patted her bare ass with the paddle before the first spank, wondering how hard to do it and not wanting to mess up. She grunted with the first hard stroke and gasped with the second, her breath catching in her throat with the initial sting and then releasing through her grimacing face. It was way more serious than in the woods. The paddle made a cracking sound when it hit her skin. It wasn't sexy like it was when I fantasized about it. It wasn't light or fun or playful. It was scary, because I was afraid of doing the wrong thing. I was glad when I got to ten and could stop. By then, she was crying, but I don't think it was really because it hurt. It wasn't that kind of crying. It was more like a paddling was just the sort of thing that could make you cry.

We cuddled on the couch for a while, without kissing or anything. She held me with one of her hands; with the other she gently stroked the red skin on her behind. I could tell by the way she laid her head on my shoulder that I hadn't done anything wrong. I stroked her hair and she didn't seem so scary anymore. When I kissed the top of her head, she began to cry harder, as if she had thought of something that made her really sad. Maybe her whole smart-mouth attitude was just to protect her from feeling like this. She sniffled and I handed her a Kleenex from the end table. She sat up and blew her nose. Then she looked up at me, using her thumb and pinkie to pull her hair, wet with tears, back from her face.

"Did you like the paddle?" she asked, trying to be light. She smiled underneath her sniffles.

"I dunno. Did you?"

"Goddamn it, Brian. Don't you ever say anything?" She started crying again.

"I'm sorry. It's just…" What I had meant to say was that I didn't think it was really about whether or not I liked the paddle.

"Yeah, Brian. I love the fucking paddle. I love it so much. That's why I wanted you to spank me with it. Because I have this thing about having Daddy spank me, and I keep hoping to find someone who'll be this crazy Daddy fantasy thing for me and call me 'Sugar,' and it's just hopeless so I don't know why I do it."

Why was she mad at me?

"You want me to pretend I'm your daddy?"

"No, shithead. I want someone to be the man I always fantasize about, but if you have to ask, you can't be him."

"Oh."

If I wasn't doing too well at this, that's because this wasn't the sort of thing that happened to me. I had only heard about this stuff from other people. Sex games that go too far; girls who spill their guts to you: I'd heard about this stuff, but it didn't happen in my world. I was outside of it, almost as if I were watching it on TV or in a movie.

I wondered how this would sound to the guys in a dorm room drinking beer. At least now I would have a story to tell that wasn't a complete lie. Except that this wasn't the kind of thing that you told people about. I had finally made it to the land of sex and drama, only to learn that you didn't do things like this just so you could impress your friends.

She started to cry even more.

"Hey," I said and held her to me. "Hey."

But she wouldn't be soothed. I looked out the window, dumbfounded, a bare-bottomed girl beside herself in my lap. She was bawling so hard that she was choking. I thought of something and at first there was no way in hell I was going to do it, but then I couldn't stand it any longer so I did.

"Sugar?"

She stopped mid-sob and looked up at me. It wasn't a look I had ever seen on anyone's face before.

"You need another paddling, uh, Sugar."

I said it as a statement but also as a question. She could veto it. She could tell me it wasn't working for her, that it was making it worse, but she didn't.

"Yes...Daddy."

The spell was cast. Her voice wasn't smart or sarcastic, and mine wasn't scared or timid.

"You know what happens when you get in trouble, don't you, Sugar?"

"Yes, Daddy."

She got up and then lay facedown over my lap.

"Daddy's going to give his little girl thirty swats with the paddle now."

"No, Daddy, I'm too sore. You just spanked me. That's too many."

"You're going to get whatever I say, Sugar. You know better than to argue. You'll get extra strokes if you're not careful."

"But Daddy…" and she started to cry again, only this time it was different. She was crying as if the worst thing in the world was the spanking she was going to get. It was like she was little again, before it all felt so hopeless, before you were too scared to tell someone what you were thinking. I still don't know what to do about those things, but at that moment, I knew exactly what to do. I raised the paddle up in the air and brought it down hard.

"One…"

N. T. MORLEY

YOUR WISH IS MY COMMAND

CHRIST," PARKER SAID, almost under her breath. "I'm not sure I want to do this."

"You've got to be fucking kidding me," Vanessa answered, in a pique.

"No," snapped Parker, emotion building. "I *can't* do it."

"It was your idea!"

Parker was blushing, but then she'd been blushing for an hour. She looked at her friend hopelessly. Vanessa gave her a glare that would have melted chromium steel.

Vanessa's lithe body—raised to six feet on the heels of the boots she was wearing—was garbed in a rubber catsuit so tight that it showed every detail of her body. You could even see her nipples through the rubber—though part of that was because the breast cups had sculpted nipples. Vanessa had actually had to shave herself to get into the damn thing, it was so tight, and she'd complained about it endlessly to Parker.

Vanessa was in no mood for a reluctant partner. "You are not backing out of this," she snarled, her face livid with anger. "I'm sweating my fucking tits off, Park-ker, and you are not backing out of this, Park-ker!" Vanessa always accentuated both syllables of her best friend's name when she was really pissed off. And she was pissed with good reason—it *was* Parker's idea to dress up like this for the charity auction. And of course Vanessa was sweating more than Parker—no wonder she was bitchy. "And my fucking feet are killing me—who the hell wears six-inch heels, anyway?"

"Oh, I think they're hot," said Parker nervously, trying to change the subject.

Vanessa responded by tapping the leather riding crop on her palm a few times—and then whacking it so hard that Parker jumped. If Parker couldn't manage to weasel out of it, Vanessa was going to do horrible things to Parker's ass—and in front of a hundred screaming frat boys.

Well, they weren't all frat boys. The AIDS charity auction was sponsored by a slew of campus fraternities, but it was also sponsored by Lambda House, the campus gay–lesbian organization. A lot of the frat brothers had declined to work alongside their more Greek-inclined associates. But some had put their prejudices aside and volunteered for the auction, no doubt thinking it would make the chicks think they were "sensitive."

The booming voice of Big Teddy Gumdrop, DJ at the town's only gay bar, was introducing the act right before Parker and Vanessa.

"Let's have a big hand for LaKisha Swanson, wearing a dress made of condoms!"

There was a round of halfhearted applause as LaKisha strolled out onto the runway. Teddy gushed gloriously about the condom-dress—"Made of *both lubricated and unlubricated* condoms, so you can let those dirty mouths wander—cuts down on time running to the medicine chest!" He got some scattered laughs.

Jesus. A dress made of condoms. That was maybe the only thing Parker could think of that was more humiliating than what she was wearing: a plaid, rubber schoolgirl's skirt—micro-mini was understating the matter—and a white latex blouse that hung open, showing her black leather bra. Her hair was put up in those goofy pigtails, sticking out obscenely from the top of her head. If they followed the plan—which Parker was trying to figure out some way to avoid—when the announcer called their names they were going to walk out on the runway to the sound of Nine Inch Nails' "Closer," and prance around for thirty seconds before Vanessa forcibly bent Parker over the high stool thoughtfully provided, then whipped the living tar out of her.

Well, that wasn't the idea. It was supposed to be just a couple of whacks—gentle ones, Vanessa had promised. But from the way Vanessa was tapping that riding crop, Parker wasn't entirely sure her best friend wasn't going to go a little overboard. *Maybe a lot overboard,* Parker thought as Vanessa scowled.

"You were the one who came up with this whole idea," said the annoyed Vanessa, as if in answer. "You were the one who thought it would be really fun to dress up like schoolgirl and dominatrix and—"

"Vanessa, I know."

"—go out in front of a million horny frat boys and every fag on campus and—"

"Vanessa, I know!"

"—lift your skirt and let me spank the shit out of you—all in the name of safer sex, mind you, good clean fun for the betterment of society, something I guess you read in a left-wing sociology textbook—"

"Vanessa! I know! I know it was my idea! I'm just a little freaked out, is all! Do we have to do the spanking thing?"

"Yes," growled Vanessa. "We have to do the spanking thing. What else are we going to do if I don't spank you?"

"I don't know—dance or something?"

"Dominatrixes and schoolgirls do not dance," said Vanessa primly. "We'll look like fucking Michael Madsen in *Reservoir Dogs*."

"You're a good dancer," said Parker weakly.

"Flattery will get you nowhere."

"Couldn't I just, like, get down on my knees in front of you or something?" The instant Parker had said it, she'd regretted it. Oh, *that* was a fucking bright idea.

To Parker's horror and dismay, Vanessa's face brightened. "Hey, that's a great idea. That would be hot. Total schoolgirl submission thing. The frat boys will love it. You sure you don't mind?"

"I—"

"We're going to have to sit out there for a while anyway, when they're auctioning off the outfits. You can just stay on your knees in front of me the whole time. That would be so hot!"

"Oh God, look, I wasn't thinking about that—"

"Sold! To the gentleman in the pink tux! Please see the cashier, Pinkie. Ladies and gentlemen—"

Parker felt as if a knife had just been jabbed into her guts. Her head swam.

"Calm down," whispered Vanessa, her voice cutting through the haze of fear.

"Now we have a very special act for you, something I'm sure all you fraternity pledges will drool over! Showing the many faces of latex, we've got—"

"Oh God, oh God…" Parker muttered, feeling she was going to throw up. She just knew it.

"Mistress Vanessa and her Slave Girl, Parker, displaying latex fetishwear from Gothic Dreams!"

As they strolled out onto the runway, they were met with shocked faces, horrified and disgusted at the vileness of Parker's half-naked body and the scandalous nature of her outfit. Frat boys and gay boys alike started screaming and throwing things—pelting Parker with garbage. Parker felt her stomach seizing up as Vanessa tightened her grip on the leash—and then she passed out.

"Parker! *Parker!* He called our names! We have to go out there."

"What?" Parker was in a daze.

"It's time. We have to get out there." Then Vanessa leaned close and whispered into Parker's ear: "I'll be gentle."

Maybe it was the warm feeling of Vanessa's breath on Parker's ear. Maybe it was the way Vanessa spoke to her—with a feeling of closeness, tenderness. Maybe it was just that in the vortex of terror she was experiencing, Parker felt so dazed that she let her eyes wander slowly up and down the length of Vanessa's rubber-sheathed body, and realized, in a flash, that her best friend looked fucking *hot*.

"Yes, Mistress," Parker heard herself saying, terror surging up as she curtsied, the way Vanessa had taught her. "Your wish is my command. I hear and obey."

"Don't be a smart-ass," said Vanessa, and swatted Parker on the ass.

"Here they are!" said Teddy, laughing a little nervously. "Girls, we were beginning to wonder about you—we thought you got started on your act a little early, hah hah hah…"

Parker's head spun at the sudden wave of silence that swept over the auditorium as Vanessa led her out onto the stage. Vanessa strolled with power in her gait, her long legs making Parker practically run just to keep up. How the hell did Vanessa walk like that in six-inch heels? Parker was surprised to be struck by her sudden curiosity—maybe Vanessa had had more practice than she let on.

The silence overwhelmed her. Parker felt a surge of fear—they hated her. They despised her. They were disgusted.

Then the cheers started. The sounds washed over Parker and Vanessa as they grew in volume. In only a few seconds, Parker's ears were hurting.

Vanessa stepped aside and displayed her schoolgirl, posing with her tits sticking out—sculpted nipples and everything—as Parker curtsied again, bringing a series of whoops and howls from the crowd. She curtsied twice more as Teddy spoke.

"That's right, give it up for Mistress Vanessa and Slave Girl Parker. You college kids have it so easy! Back in my day, we *never* had dominatrixes and latex schoolgirls on campus, just acid and 'ludes!"

The crowd's cheers rose in volume—whether because of the curtsies Parker had given or because of Teddy's cheesy drug quip, Parker couldn't say. And she didn't care.

Her eyes were dazzled by the bright lights, but she could see the guys and girls in the audience howling with laughter, cheering and pointing at her. For an instant she wondered if they were laughing at her or with her, and then she realized that it didn't matter—they were captivated, unable to look away, and that was what mattered.

"Ladies and gentlemen, if there are any of you like that out there, Mistress Vanessa tells me that Slave Girl Parker has been a very, very, verrrrrrrrry bad, bad, bad slave girl. Isn't that right, Slave Girl Parker?"

Parker blinked as Teddy shoved the microphone in front of her mouth.

"I said, isn't that right, Slave Girl Parker?"

"Y—yes," said Parker nervously. "I've been a bad, bad girl."

On cue, the sound system started playing Fiona Apple's song—as if they couldn't have seen that one coming a friggin' mile away, but the crowd erupted in cheers again anyway. Simple minds, simple pleasures.

"And what do we do with bad, bad slave girls, Slave Girl Parker?" giggled Teddy.

"Uhhhhh…" Parker groped for the words.

"We spank the living shit out of them," said Vanessa as she grabbed the microphone from Teddy, her voice low and husky—a voice Parker had never heard from her best friend before. "Isn't that right, Parker?"

Parker put her lips to the already spit-slick microphone, and managed to say, "Yes, Mistress. Your wish is my command."

This time the cheers were so loud they made the microphone feed back.

The riding crop came up, and down again. Parker jumped, but Vanessa was just tapping her shoulder. Vanessa spoke into the microphone: "Bend over, Slave Girl!"

The crowd went crazy with screams, laughs, and cheers as Parker nervously turned around and then stepped up to the stool that had been arranged for just that purpose. She had known it was coming, but still she wasn't prepared for the wave of fear she felt as she slowly bent over, placing her belly above the seat of the stool.

Damn it! She was too tall! She couldn't lean on the stool properly.

"Spread your legs," hissed Vanessa, covering the microphone with her hand—but then the microphone started to feed back again. Parker didn't move, so Vanessa spoke into the microphone this time: "Spread your legs, Slave Girl Parker."

They'd tried it with this stool before, and it was too low for her if she kept her legs together. Had she really agreed to fucking spread her legs in front of all these screaming frat boys? She must have been smoking crack. Parker's head spun as she tried to figure out how she could get out of it now. But she couldn't.

"I said, spread your legs, Slave Girl Parker!" snapped Vanessa into the microphone. "Are you disobeying your mistress?"

She stuck the microphone into Parker's face, and Parker squeaked, "No, Mistress. Your wish is my command."

And then she spread her legs, and the crowd erupted in cheers and catcalls.

Parker spread her legs wider, and snuggled down onto the stool, listening as Vanessa gave her the next order.

"Now lift your skirt, Slave Girl Parker."

Oh God, oh God, oh God. She couldn't do that! She was wearing underwear, sure, but what difference did that make? Besides, it was latex underwear—she was sure the crowd would be able to see everything.

"Lift your skirt!"

"Yes, Mistress. Your wish is my command."

Parker's hands were shaking as she reached back and lifted the plaid, latex skirt. The crowd howled.

Parker felt more exposed than she had ever been before—because she was. She was standing in front of hundreds of frat boys, legs spread wide, her skirt lifted and only the thinnest, skimpiest latex panties between her and them. Between her vulnerable, exposed body and theirs.

God, what had made her think of that?

At least she wasn't wet. She was much too scared to be wet. Much too freaked out. It was just an act, after all. Just a game. It had nothing to do with sexual interest. Parker knew she was straight, and besides, even if she hadn't been, Vanessa was, too. And none of these guys would have wanted to fuck Parker anyway.

"Damn!" giggled Teddy. "That's enough to make me straight— almost. Wouldn't you boys like to take that home?"

The crowd erupted again in cheers and shouted encouragement, and Parker realized with horror that she could hear feminine voices among the shouts—"Work it, girl," and "Pussy power!" in particular.

Parker wondered for the hundredth time how she had gotten into this.

"Are you ready for your spanking, little girl?" Vanessa's voice had a quality to it that Parker didn't recognize—a commanding nature that made her shiver.

"Yes, Mistress," she said once more. "Your wish is my command."

WHACK! Parker jumped at the loud sound—and heard herself screaming.

"If you think that's hard, little girl, wait until you find out what happens when you don't clean up your room!" It was Vanessa, laughing cruelly, sneering down at Parker as the schoolgirl looked over her shoulder at her best friend. But Parker realized that her ass didn't hurt—Vanessa had barely hit her at all. Scarcely tapped her. She'd just held the microphone so close to Parker's ass that the crop-crack had sounded like a gunshot. How the hell had the crazy bitch thought of that trick?

Then she did it again, and even though she knew it was coming this time, Parker jumped once more. The crack rang out like a gunshot through the auditorium, and the crowd roared. The microphone whined, and Vanessa put it to her lips again.

"Say 'thank you, Mistress,' " she purred, and Parker felt the microphone against her lips again, slick with spit.

"Thank you, Mistress," Parker heard herself saying, her voice as much a purr as Vanessa's. She couldn't be wet—she was much too freaked out to be wet. Maybe she was just sweating.

"Spread your legs wider, Slave Girl Parker," ordered Vanessa. Parker hadn't realized that when she'd jumped, she'd snuggled her thighs back together. Now, without hesitating for even an instant, she spread her legs wide, pulled her skirt up further, and listened to the crowd cheering.

WHACK! She wasn't wet. *WHACK!* They were all looking at her. *WHACK!* Looking at her ass, getting hard and wet as they watched her being punished in front of everybody. *In front of everybody. Is Vanessa wet, too? No, no, I'm not wet. I can't be wet. I'm totally straight, and this doesn't even interest me, it's just fun to have all these guys looking at my ass. Fine, then, I'm not wet, but I wonder if Vanessa's wet. She did make that comment once about her boyfriend Todd's* Playboy *… God, could Vanessa be getting turned on by this?* Parker squirmed and whimpered into the microphone as she felt the barely-there taps on her ass—and found herself wishing, all of a sudden, that Vanessa was hitting her harder. *Not that I'd like that,* thought Parker. *But it would be more realistic. For the crowd, I mean. I wonder what that would feel like? It feels kind of good being hit lightly like this—I wonder what it would be like to be spanked hard—really, really hard…?*

"One last time," cooed Vanessa into the microphone. "Beg me for it, Slave Girl Parker."

No way. Vanessa couldn't possibly be getting turned on by this. She was just acting for the crowd. Parker's mind was working so furiously that she almost forgot her line. Finally it came to her: "Please, Mistress, may I have another?"

Then it happened. Vanessa brought the crop down, hard this time, so hard Parker didn't just jump; she practically screamed too. Which was probably more about the fact that Parker had decided, this time, to obediently lift her ass for her mistress's crop, and had done so just as Vanessa brought the crop down. As a result, Vanessa had nailed Parker's pussy dead-on, right between her swollen lips—swollen from heat, of course, being imprisoned in the latex panties, and spread apart only from the tightness of the unbreathing garment, of course—and the pain exploded through Parker's body. Even through the latex panties, it felt like Vanessa had just given Parker a stiff kick from those pointy-toed boots right in Parker's unfortunate cleft.

Vanessa handed Teddy the microphone and leaned close to Parker's face, so close Parker could smell her sweet breath, feel it warm on her face. Parker took a deep breath, shaking her ass to cheers from the audience. Vanessa's bitch-persona had turned into the worried best friend in an instant—as soon as she realized she'd missed Parker's ass and hit her pussy. "Oh God," she murmured, "sorry, sorry, sorry—oh, I'm so sorry, baby, I didn't mean to hit you there—oh, God, are you okay?"

Through stars and whirling pain, Parker felt a trickle of moisture escape the crotch of her latex panties and run down her thigh. *They can see it*, she thought as she savored the pain radiating outward from her tortured pussy. *It's just sweat, but they think it's something else. It's so hot under these lights, it's so hot in these panties. They can all see how wet I am—dripping wet, gushing down my thighs. God, that hurt like a motherfucker. Why didn't she watch where she was hitting me? Right on the clit—she hit me right on the goddamn pussy. Oh God, I've got to get backstage and masturbate.*

"No," moaned Parker softly into Vanessa's too-close face. "I think I'll be fine."

A horrified look crossed Vanessa's face, as Parker stared into her eyes. She had never really noticed how beautiful her friend was—except in the jealous way that came from Vanessa's getting all the guys. But now…it didn't bother her at all.

"Ooooh, that's gotta hurt!" Teddy was laughing. "All right, now that our slave girl's had her spanking, you two sit there and do your thing while we finish this little bit of business, then you two sizzling-hot girls can go backstage and slide right out of those outfits—hey, there's a thought, now, guys!" The crowd erupted in cheers. "And yes, you naughty boys, you get *these* outfits, fresh off our little sluts' bodies. Let's start the bidding!"

Obediently, Parker got off the stool, looked into Vanessa's eyes, saw the fear and discomfort there. What Parker did next shocked her. Tenderly, to screams from the crowd that drowned out all previous cheers, Slave Girl Parker stood up on her tiptoes and placed a kiss on her mistress's mouth, not even closing her lips when she felt the full swell of Vanessa's lips against hers, and lingering when she felt the electricity flare through her. Vanessa didn't kiss back, though she didn't pull away. The crowd's shouts were deafening.

Meekly, Vanessa sat down on the stool, her latex-sheathed thighs pressed tightly together.

And meekly, Parker said, "Your wish is my command, Mistress," and lowered herself to her knees and put her head in her best friend's lap.

The two outfits were soon auctioned off together for an obscene sum. Some silver-spoon frat boy would have a hell of a charge to explain on his father's AmEx bill next month—"No, really, Dad, it was a charity auction. For…uh…starving children in Uganda. Yeah, organized by the Campus AIDS Project."

But not before he and his friends put this outfit to good use, Parker thought wickedly.

When they got backstage, Parker felt sure she was going to be able to wait until she got to her dorm room, but she wasn't. The second she stepped inside the little backstage bathroom, pulled down her latex panties, and sat down on the toilet, she started. She didn't even know she was doing it, really, but suddenly she was rubbing her clit, sliding one finger down to her pussy between strokes. Sliding one finger, then two, inside her, discovering only then that she really *was* wet—wetter than she'd ever been or ever thought she could be—and it wasn't merely sweat, though there was plenty of that, too.

But what was really embarrassing was that Vanessa wouldn't have suspected anything if the first orgasm hadn't just primed Parker's need for more—and it took her five minutes to come, the second time, rubbing her clit in big circles and leaning back on the toilet tank so she could work a finger into her pussy. She came so hard she cried out, which sounded like a sob, and then she heard Vanessa knocking fervently on the door.

"Are you all right?"

"Yeah…" said Parker nervously, her voice shaky as the orgasm echoed inside her.

"Do you need help? Do you want me to come in?"

Jesus, thought Parker. *Do I ever.*

"No," she sighed. "I'll be out in a minute."

Vanessa needed Parker's help getting out of the catsuit, which had decided to stick to every inch of her skin. Parker even had to unzip the crotch and peel the latex down off Vanessa's ass, which didn't help matters a bit.

But she didn't say a word, even when she was bent over Vanessa's upthrust buttocks, even when the thought occurred to her that a real slave girl would have shown her submission by licking her mistress's ass in front of the whole crowd.

"Pull harder," said Vanessa, and Parker did. The latex suit came free with a wet noise, and Vanessa giggled.

"Our reputation is sealed," said Vanessa miserably, dipping her french fry in ketchup. "We're the sluts of the whole campus. I hadn't expected to attain that honor until my junior year at least."

"There are worse things, aren't there?" said Parker, lazily toying with a fry.

"And the lesbos. I swear, next time we go to a party, everyone there is going to expect us to make out for them. Nice fucking touch, pervert."

"Oh, come on, we didn't do anything they can't see on MTV."

"Yeah, right," snorted Vanessa. "Except we gave it to them live."

"Come on. Guys will be begging us for dates."

Now a crowd of frat rats came into the diner, spotted Vanessa and Parker, and recognized them instantly. They started pointing at the two girls and laughing.

"See?" said Vanessa. "We'll never live this down."

"Come on, we're celebrities. We're heroes."

"Yeah, especially to those dykes in the front row."

"So? I think it's pretty cool we had the guts to go through with it."

"Oh yeah, right! You're the one who almost chickened out. If I hadn't pushed you out there, you'd still be cowering backstage."

"And I love you for it," said Parker, and Vanessa looked shocked. To defuse the statement, Parker stuck out her tongue at Vanessa, and the tension dissolved into giggles.

Suddenly, a frat boy appeared at Parker's elbow. Vanessa looked at him angrily.

"You were the girls—"

"Yes," snapped Vanessa meanly. "That was us. What do you want?"

"I was wondering…" the frat boy said, holding out a napkin and a ballpoint pen to Parker. "Could I have your autograph?"

Vanessa started laughing hysterically, but Parker didn't think it was very funny. In fact, she thought it was very fucking cool. Which is why Parker just smiled demurely, looked at the guy—who was hella cute—and said, "Your wish is my command."

She took the napkin and signed her name, while Vanessa laughed her ass off.

MO

CRACK THE CODE. My digital sex life with Mo was fun, but for the most part, silly. I soon got tired of it; it was all right when you were bored and on the computer, but the novelty could only last for so long.

> *What are you doing right now?* Mo IM'ed me.
>
> *Nothing,* I wrote back. *Just sitting here.*
>
> *Why don't you come over?*
>
> *Where do you live?*

She gave me her address. I was leery at first, wondering if I was being set up. For all I knew, Mo could be a guy. She did tell me she was Asian, nineteen, and that people said she was pretty. What the hell; I believed her, and went to her place.

She was fortunate to be living in the apartments and not the dorms, for an undergraduate, but still she shared the place with two other young women (whom I had not met yet). Mo greeted me in a long white terry-cloth robe. Like most kids at the university, she didn't get out of bed until afternoon. She was an exquisite young woman, and part of my delight was that she was indeed a young woman, and real at that. She was Asian, as she had said, and had dark eyes, brown skin, and long straight black hair. She was tall and slender and she smiled at me at the door and said, "Hello," and let me in. "So," she said, "you're WmGibson."

"WmGibson" was the screen name I used online—a bad one at that, all the cyberpunk connotations laid right out.

"Actually," I said, "my name is Nick."

"You said."

"I did?"

"Yeah."

"Nicky," I said.

"I like 'WmGibson,' " Mo said.

The apartment smelled of young women and looked like they lived there. I felt awkward, being older than Mo. I knew that many of the graduate students who were teaching assistants slept with their freshmen students—it was all par for the course. But I wasn't a T.A., and Mo wasn't one of my students. I was getting ahead of myself, anyway—how did I know that something of a sexual nature was going to occur between Mo and me? Maybe she had just invited me over to be friendly?

Mo offered me something to drink, and I said milk would be nice. She laughed at that, and said, "Don't you want a beer?"

"Not now," I said.

"I have milk," she said.

She got me a glass of milk and she had a soda. We talked some; it was small talk. Her robe kept falling opening, giving me a glimpse of her cleavage, but each time she'd quickly close it. I was falling in lust. Mo never wiped away the sultry grin she maintained, and I couldn't read what was in her small dark eyes, often covered by strands of her jet-black hair. I detected something insidious. I didn't know if I should make a move or not.

"Let's get online," she suggested, "and tell everyone you're here. That should stir up some gossip."

It didn't sound exciting to me, but I said, "Why not?" Mo lived to be online; she was a true William Gibson character in the flesh— bright, Asian, Net-savvy. I asked about her heritage, and she said her family had come from Korea.

She took me to her bedroom, one of three in the unit. It was small and cluttered, with a single bed, a desk, and a Macintosh computer. It smelled feminine. Clothes were strewn all over the floor—skirts, jeans, blouses, bras, panties.

She logged into one of the chatrooms we both frequented; sure enough, people we knew were there, both on-campus and all over the globe.

Guess who is here in my room? Mo typed. *WmGibson! :^)*

Some people said hello to me, some said they didn't believe it.

"Say hello," Mo said to me, getting up from her desk.

I sat at the desk. Mo perched on the edge of her bed, which was very close to the desk.

Hey everyone, I typed. *It is me, WmGibson, aka Nicky Bayless, and I am here with Mo.*

Answers were like so:

No way!

Kiss Mo!

Jerk!

It's Mo fooling again.

I felt silly typing, *No, it's really me.*

This is when Mo slipped her foot between my legs. First she guided her naked foot, with clean, well-clipped nails, up my leg, leaned back on the bed, and got her foot into my crotch. This wasn't an easy thing to do, as I had my torso half-turned in the chair. I turned some more.

She sprang up and came to me. She sat in my lap. She reached for the keyboard and typed: *Guess what I'm going? Rubbing WmGibson's cock and balls with my left foot!*

She added: *I'm now trying to stick my big toe up his asshole. His asshole is resistant, but my toe is getting in there.*

I laughed, and she laughed.

As the chatroom clamor went on, I touched Mo—her back, her neck, her breasts. She stood, and we embraced. She ran her fingers through my hair and it felt nice. I kissed her chest where the robe opened.

"I haven't showered in three days," she told me. "I must be gross."

"No," I said, though I could smell and taste her sweat.

I started to stand, to kiss her. She pushed me back down on the chair.

"I don't kiss," she said.

"What?"

"Anyone."

"Why?"

"I hate saliva," she said. "Mouths, tongues—yuck."

We continued to embrace and touch. I pulled at the sash of her robe.

She said, "What do you think you're doing, little boy?"

"I want to see your body," I said. "You won't let me kiss you, so let me see your body."

"Only for a second," she said.

She opened her robe, still in my arms, and revealed her young, beautiful frame. Medium-sized breasts with dark nipples, an "outie" belly button, a thick patch of black pubic hair. She then closed her robe and smiled and said, *"There,* you've seen it."

"Kiss me."

"No way."

I pulled her to me, my face pressing between her covered breasts. She continued to run her fingers through my hair.

"Play on the Net," she said. "I'm going to take a shower."

"Now?"

"I *need* a shower."

She left me there, at her desk, and went into the bathroom. I heard the water run. I logged her account off, and logged onto mine, getting back on the same chatroom channel.

Hey, someone named Nexus said, *are you really at Mo's place?*

Yes, I replied.

Coolio.

I was getting all the signals wrong. Mo was naked in the shower, I could see from my chair; I saw the hot water hitting her brown body, rolling down it. I logged off, got up, and went in.

"Is that you?" Mo said from the shower.

There was a lot of steam. I said, "Yes."

"It's about time," she said. "Get naked and join me."

I got naked and joined her.

We spent a good twenty minutes cleaning one another with a bar of soap, shampooing each other's hair, and touching each other's sex. I took every opportunity I could get to feel her body—her neck, her chest, her breasts, her stomach, her ass, her cunt. She let me finger her clit, but wouldn't let me slide my finger in; each time I tried, she said, "No, not yet." Not yet? And she still wouldn't kiss me on the lips; she allowed me to kiss other parts of her body, but not the lips. She took my hard cock in her hand, stroked it, and took it in both hands. I made myself not come. We got out of the shower and dried each other off. Naked, we went back to her bedroom. I pushed her toward the bed.

"I said I will not kiss you," she said.

"I know," I said, and put my mouth on her tits.

I reached for her cunt. She sat up. I lay on the bed, rubbed her back.

"You should know something," she said. "I'm a virgin."

"I've heard that before," I said, and stifled a sad…a very sad laugh.

"What?" she said, and just when I thought she would tell me I could fuck her in the ass, Mo said, "I swallow."

"What's that?"

"I can suck like a crazy machine," she said.

"Show me," I said.

"I want to show you," she said, and did. She went down on my cock. She wasted no time, and soon had the whole thing in her mouth. She cupped my balls in her hand, squeezing just a little too hard. After the whole shower bit, I was ready to explode, and explode I did, several huge spurts of semen, which she swallowed completely.

"Yum," she said. "Reminds me, I'm hungry. You want to go get something to eat?"

"I want to eat *you*," I said.

"Not now, later," she said. She stood, and went to her closet. "I need food. I don't want to eat on campus."

"There's plenty of places to go," I said.

"Okay," she said. "Don't watch me dress."

"I just like looking at you."

"I *don't* like people watching me dress. Go get your clothes on."

I went to the bathroom and retrieved my clothes, like a good boy.

We went to get pizza a few miles off campus. She ordered a beer and wasn't carded.

She leaned forward, voice low. "I can still taste your come in my mouth. The back of my mouth, really. You just pumped your come in my mouth and I don't know anything about you. Don't you think that's kinda weird, on my part?"

"I'm getting hard again."

"Good. I like guys who're always hard."

"Tell me about you," I said.

"I like sucking dick," she said. "I like to swallow. I could swallow all day."

"I'm twenty-eight," I said.

"Nice."

"Grad student."

"Nice."

"I write things."

"Nice."

"But you know all this."

"Yes."

"So what do you want to know?"

"Do you have a girlfriend?"

"No."

"Do you want me to be your girlfriend?"

"Yes."

"Will you marry me?"

"I don't know you."

"Will you *marry* me?"

"Yes," I said.

"Tonight?"

"We could drive to Vegas."

"Mo Bayless. Sounds funny."

"Let's do it," I said.

"I'd give up my virginity for the man who'd marry me."

"We can be in Vegas before midnight," I said.

She said, "Many guys wanna marry me."

"I bet."

"I have a lot of boyfriends."

"I bet," I said, and asked, "Do you swallow them all?"

She said, "Yes."

"Oh."

"I bet you have girlfriends."

"Women come and go in my life," I said. "Dark entries."

"And I'm just another," she said.

"Tell me about Maureen."

"Mo."

"Oh?"

"I hate 'Maureen.' "

"Mo."

"Mo has nowhere to go," she said, softly.

"What?"

She eyed me. "My parents would never approve of you."

"I'm too old."

"Too white."

"I see."

"I have to marry a nice Korean man—"

"I could fake it," I said.

"—someday."

"But not today?"

"Today," she said, "I'd marry you."

"Let's do it."

"You just want my pussy."

"I want *you.*"

"Are you still hard?"

"Very."

"I want to swallow you again," she said. "Maybe for dessert?"

"Let's eat fast."

"Behavioral science," Mo said.

"What?"

"My major. For now."

"How am *I* behaving?"

"Too nice," she said.

"What should I do, to not be so nice?"

"Grab me by the hair. Force me to suck your dick."

"Here?"

"Sure."

When we were done eating, and in my car, I grasped her hair, hard. I tried to kiss her.

"Don't kiss me," she said, a hand propped against my chest.

"Dammit," I said.

"Make me suck your dick. I have these elaborate fantasies that I'll tell you about someday."

I took my cock out, grabbed her head, and pushed her down on it. I closed my eyes, enjoying the sensation of her blow job. I came in her mouth for the second time that night.

I took Mo home, and there I met her two roommates, both of whom had short hair and were nineteen or twenty, young.

"Just another guy," I said to Mo when we got into her room, referring to her roommates' looks.

"Do you care?"

"No," I said.

"Do you want your dick sucked more?"

"Yes," I said.

We undressed in the dark, and lay on the bed, where she took my cock back into her mouth. I wanted her, too; I told her this.

Mo said, "I'd like your face in my pussy."

I was quick to get between her legs. Now I had her cunt before me, the fresh smell of it, and I licked it. I spread it open. I couldn't admire, in the dark, what I knew must have been the beauty of a virgin twat, but I could taste it, and it was the sweetest cunt I've ever had on my tongue, my lips, my mouth. Mo squirmed with delight, and made enough loud sounds that I knew her roommates were getting an earful. I moved a finger to her opening, and was surprised she let me do this. I slid the finger in. Mo's body tensed all over, and began to shake. "That's it, Nicky," she said, "finger-fuck that kitty," and I did, sliding it in and out, my tongue pressed and lapping against her clit the whole time. Mo's shaking became almost frightening, but intriguing and fun at the same time; and she came with such a shrill cry I'm sure it echoed all across the campus.

I kissed her belly button, my lips wet with her sex. I moved up to kiss her mouth, but she looked away. I moved up still more, so that my cock was at her lips. She took it. My hands were against the wall by the bed, balancing my body, so that I was able to move my cock in and out of her mouth with the motion of my hips, fucking her pretty Asian face. Looking down, all I could see was the silhouette of her hair, and a slight whiteness of her eyes, as she was looking up at me. Mo's hands grabbed my ass, pulling me, making me fuck her mouth deeper. She squeezed and rubbed my ass, and one fingernailed digit moved to touch my asshole. I was a piston, going in and out of her mouth, and soon I too let out a loud groan (maybe too loud, maybe wanting her roommates to hear) and came in Mo's mouth a third time that night.

I came in her mouth a fourth time a few hours later, waking up to her sucking me off. It took me a good while to get there that fourth time, but she didn't seem to mind, and I enjoyed every minute, every second.

It was awkward sleeping in that single bed with her; we had to be close and entwined. Sleeping with someone else, I usually like room. But it was nice. Her smell, her body, her hair, her flesh was always on me. I felt her pubes against my leg. She slept well, but I didn't. I never sleep well in a new environment. I looked at her in the night, pondered on her beauty, basked in the comfort of being with her.

In the morning, we sixty-nined, she on top of me; I licked her from cunt to asshole as she kept my cock deep in her mouth. She didn't come, but I did.

She had to get ready to go to class, and I had to go home. I had nothing to do there, though. I tried talking her into skipping class.

"Kiss me good-bye," she said.

I kissed her, gently, on the lips.

"That's no kiss," Mo said.

"You said you hated kissing."

"I say that to all strangers."

"I'm not a stranger?" I asked.

"After last night…?" she said.

We kissed for a good five minutes. Then I left.

GRETA CHRISTINA

THIS WEEK

COME CLOSER.

Here's what it is this week. A girl, a college student, is being spanked by her college professor. She's young, nineteen or twenty, young enough to be in college, but old enough to have some sexual knowledge. He's older, of course, probably in his forties, dressed casually but with dignity, a trim beard with a hint of gray. She is dressed, not in the schoolgirl outfit of porn cliché, but in regular modern clothing that merely implies the schoolgirl look: a short skirt with a flare, a simple blouse, white panties. The white panties are important. She is bent over his lap with her skirt pulled up and her panties pulled down, and he is spanking her with his hand.

Here's how they got there. I think of the girl as the instigator of the scenario. I think of her sitting in this man's class: admiring him, becoming excited by his ideas and his authority and his ease with his body. I think of her feeling flustered in his presence: not stupid, but young, and acutely self-conscious of her youth and her limitations. And I imagine these feelings coalescing into the simple image in her mind, the lap and the bare bottom and the hand coming down again and again. I think of her, not coolly deciding to act on her thoughts, but doing it impulsively, not even entirely consciously; just coming to him after class for help and advice, putting herself in his path, waiting to see what happens next.

Now. I imagine her going to his house after a test, a test on which she had done fine but could have done better. She goes to his house, dressed only somewhat on purpose in the short skirt and simple blouse and white panties. She goes to his house, apparently upset about her less-than-ideal test score, telling him that she clearly needs more help. She works herself into an agitation, a frustration about her academic performance that even she half-believes. At the same time, she's deliberately, or semideliberately, being provocative, displaying her body, putting herself in poses both seductive and submissive. She talks about how lazy she is, how little self-discipline she has, how she needs external discipline to succeed—and she drops something on the floor and turns away from him to pick it up. She says she can't achieve her best unless she fears being punished, says a B+ grade isn't enough punishment to drive her to excel—and she bends over his desk to examine a knickknack on the far side. She uses the word *punishment* again and again, and she keeps finding ways and reasons to turn away from him and bend over.

He's not an idiot. He's an adult, a middle-aged man of the world, and he can see what she wants. He wants it, too; she's a lovely girl, she makes him feel powerful and wise, and the thought of bending her over his lap makes his dick twitch. At the same time, he's not an idiot. He knows how much trouble he could get into if he's guessing wrong, or for that matter if he's guessing right. So he's careful. He asks her if she wants his help, if she wants him to provide this external motivation she's missing, to give her the punishment she needs when she fails to reach her potential. She breathes a deep breath of relief and excitement, says yes, please, can he help her? He asks again: are you sure you want this discipline, are you sure you want to be punished for not doing your best, are you sure you want me to do it? She begins to pace around the room, agitated and anxious, saying yes, yes please, that's why she came here, this is what she wants.

He looks at her face, steadily, until she stops pacing and looks at him back. They're no longer speaking in code.

Do you want this? he asks. Do you want me to punish you?

She nods. She can't say it out loud.

All right, he says. Come here.

She walks over and stands next to him. He pats his lap; he can't say the words either, and he needs her to make the gesture on her own. She stares at his lap, and at his hands, and she awkwardly kneels on the floor and crawls over his knees.

He's done this before. Not often, but more than once, and he knows what he's doing. He pulls up her skirt, not slow and sexy, not rough and impatient, but deliberate, getting the job done. He waits for her breathing to relax, then puts his hands on her waist and pulls down her panties. He moves a bit more slowly this time, but his manner is not teasing or sensual; the slowness is methodical, patient, done with calm authority. He looks at her bare bottom, listens to her breathe, waits.

He doesn't caress her—this isn't about that—but he does rest his hand on her bottom. She flinches, then realizes that he hasn't started yet, and tries to relax. He waits again. And then he begins to spank her.

His first blow is a real one. Not extreme, but she knows right away that she's being spanked. He waits, and delivers another blow, exactly the same. And then he begins to spank her in earnest. The spanking is slow, she can feel it each time his hand strikes her bottom. She begins to squirm; she's embarrassed now, self-conscious about what she's doing and how she must look, a grown woman being punished on her bare bottom like a child. And it hurts, it's hard now and it hurts, she wasn't expecting that. But she can't bring herself to say anything, she'd feel like a fool just quitting in the middle…and now it's lighter, and she thinks she can take it a little longer.

He says nothing. He concentrates on the spanking, watches her body, listens to her breathe. His cock is getting hard, it's telling him to squeeze her tits and then spank her as hard as he can; but he ignores it, tells it to be content with her warmth and her wriggling, and he centers his attention on just how hard he's spanking her, and what exactly she's doing about it.

She's squirming harder now. She feels how warm her bottom is getting, she can picture how pink it must be by now. She's getting agitated, and confused. The hard ones make her flinch and curl up—but the light ones give her time to think, and to feel: how small she is, and how flustered; her fear of the next really hard one; her uneasy frustration when the hard ones stop; her excitement; her shame at being excited; her hips wriggling against his lap. A good hard one comes down out of nowhere, and she cries out in relief and arches her back.

He still says nothing. He looks carefully now at her arched back and clenched fists, listens to the change in her voice. He stops, pulls his hand up high, and gives her five hard smacks, very hard, as fast as he can.

He listens as her cries of outrage subside into gasps. He considers starting again; he considers giving her a comforting pat on her pink bottom; he considers putting his hand between her legs. He's pretty sure he could do any of these things, and she'd respond. But he's nervous now, and doesn't know how far he wants this to go. So he pulls up her panties, carefully, not touching her skin. He pulls her skirt back down over her bottom, and then puts his hands behind his back.

She scrambles to her feet right away, looks down at the floor, her face red. She mumbles something—"Thank you, Professor," he thinks— and waits expectantly. "Good," he says. "That was very good." She stares at the floor for a moment, then scrambles for her things, mumbles "Thank you" again, and scurries out the door.

Here's what happens next. They meet once a week at his house. They don't discuss it, they don't make a plan; she just shows up at his door the next week at the same time, as if they had an appointment. She puts down her things, and she tells him about her schoolwork, the week's successes and failures. He congratulates her on her achievements, and then he analyzes her failures, explaining exactly what she did wrong and why it matters. And then he pats his lap.

It always has to be a punishment. She can't simply walk in the door and say, "Okay, let's get to the spanking." And neither can he.

They can't quite acknowledge what this is; they find it easier to think of it as instruction, discipline. Anyway, it's more exciting this way. So he begins to write tests, every week, just for her—tests for her to make mistakes on. She's a bright girl and she wants to please him; so he has to make the tests hard, hard enough that she'll miss at least one question and will need to be punished. She takes the tests very seriously, studies hard for them. She does, in fact, become a better student during this time, in all her classes, not only his. And she never misses a question on purpose. She would consider that cheating, and she is a serious student, appalled at the idea of cheating. She's always excited when he points out her errors and pats his lap; but she's always a bit disappointed as well, upset at herself for failing, and believing, at least partly, that she really is being punished, and that she deserves it.

As the weeks go by, they become more accustomed to each other. Their rhythm becomes more fluid, the ritual more detailed, the spankings longer and more intense. He begins to talk during the spankings, sometimes lecturing in detail on that week's failures, sometimes just chanting, "Bad girl! Bad! You can do better! You need discipline! You need to be punished! Punished! Bad!" He knows by now the words that set her off, the ones that make her whimper and arch her bottom in the air—and he knows the ones that make her freeze up. He knows how hard she likes to be spanked...and he knows how hard is just a little harder than she really likes, how hard is hard enough to make her feel that she's been bad, and is being punished for it.

As more weeks go by, he begins to ask if she needs any special punishment, something extra to make her pay closer attention. The first time she doesn't understand what he's getting at, she says no thank you, Professor, please just punish me. But she gets it later, alone in bed that night; and the next week when he asks again, she has her answer ready. Yes, she says. She fears that his hand isn't a hard-enough tool for serious discipline, doesn't make her fearful enough or sorry enough for what she's done. She says she needs to be punished with something harder, something that will make her more afraid to fail, something to really hurt her and make her feel ashamed. He asks her to be specific— he always needs her to ask for it, always needs it spelled out—and she's learned by now to speak up. She asks him to please spank her with a ruler, wooden or maybe metal, or with his hairbrush. He tells her to fetch his ruler—the hairbrush is too personal for him—and she goes directly to his desk and takes it out of the top drawer. She knows exactly where he keeps it.

And as still more weeks go by, the special punishments become both more elaborate and more central to the ritual. The bare-bottom over-the-knee hand spankings, once the entire reason for them being there, now become prelude—neither of them will call it foreplay—to the special punishments she asks for each week. She asks him to spank her with a rolled-up newspaper. She asks him to make her say out loud what a bad girl she is while he spanks her. She asks him to make her get on her hands and knees and kiss the floor while he spanks her. She asks him to use the ruler to spank her between her legs. She asks him to keep spanking her until she cries.

She never asks him to fuck her. He never does.

The end of the semester draws near, and both of them are a bit at a loss. She has one more year before she graduates, and no more classes with him. She starts asking about her final exam; her questions are anxious, restless. He's pretty sure he knows what she wants. With some regret he begins crafting her final. He spends every spare moment on it. He knows it has to be perfect.

She comes to his house for the final, wearing the same short skirt and simple blouse and white panties she wore for their first lesson. He hands her the test. She takes it without a word and begins immediately, working fiercely and steadily like a buzz saw. When she finishes, she hands it back and waits silently, tapping her fingers on her knee.

It's perfect, he says at last. No mistakes.

They both sit still, somewhat taken aback, sitting quietly together in the empty space that has just opened up. He guessed exactly right: this is what she wanted. But neither of them had thought about what to do next.

So, he says. No punishment today. You get punished for making mistakes. What do you get when you're perfect? Do you get a reward?

She doesn't know what to say. She'd imagined in detail how the test would go—a serious challenge, just barely within her abilities. She'd imagined her struggle to get through it, the rush of pride when he told her she was perfect. But she hadn't thought any further than that.

A reward, she says.

She could ask him to kiss her. She could ask him to fuck her. She could ask him to spend the afternoon feeding her tea and cakes and telling her how much he admires her. She could ask him to take off her shirt and play with her nipples, could tell him exactly how she wanted him to do it, and then she could make him get on his knees on the floor in front of her and lick her pussy. She could ask to sit in his lap, the lap she's been bent over so many times, and have him stroke her hair and tell her what a good girl she is. She could ask him to make her masturbate, make her lie back and spread her legs and show him how she does it, and then make her turn over onto her belly and keep masturbating, while he punished her hard on her bottom for doing it. She could ask him to give her all her special punishments over again, one after the other until she's weeping and raw, and then pin her down over his desk and push his cock into her ass. She could ask him to make the decision, to take the initiative, to, for fuck's sake, just this once, not make her come to him. She could ask him to take her over his knee, and pull up her skirt and pull down her panties, and spank her bare bottom with his hand one more time.

I'm getting all As this semester, she says. Every class. I think I'm going to make the Dean's list. And I got a special summer internship, a really good one. She tells him the name of the professor she's interning with, and he's impressed, even a little jealous. That's great news, he says. I'm really pleased to hear it.

A reward, she says. I don't know. Let me think about it. She gathers her things, says, "Thank you, Professor," in a clear voice, and quietly leaves, shutting the door behind her.

RACHEL KRAMER BUSSEL

CUNNILINGUS 101

C OUNTING THE MINUTES ticking by on the overhead clock, Rick shifted in his seat at the very back of the eight-hundred-seat lecture hall, idly flipping the pages of his Econ 101 textbook as Professor Vanderbilt droned on at the front of the class. The pompous, balding, tenured professor acted as if they should be honored to have him even set foot in front of them, let alone actually teach them something.

Who really cares about supply and demand, anyway? Rick thought.

He was eighteen, and still adjusting to campus life. Berkeley, California, was a hell of a lot different than his hometown in rural Virginia—just as he'd desired. If he really thought about it, he could cast his mind back to a time when his parents' house, with its huge backyard, rec room, cable TV, and unlimited goodies in the fridge, contained all he'd ever really needed, but now that all seemed like another era, or another person's life—pre-porn, pre-erections, pre-fantasies, pre-sex.

He considered himself barely beyond virginity, and wondered if there should be some qualifying test to pass, with losers sent back for remedial sex training. He knew he'd yet to truly taste the pleasures of female flesh, but he was sure he'd come up a winner once he got the chance—in Rick's mind, he was a cocksman par excellence.

He'd always known he was smart enough to go to a school like Cal, and in fact schoolwork was proving much easier than he'd expected. It was still a challenge, but if he kept up with the reading and diligently studied every afternoon, he'd be sure to get through his first semester with excellent grades. But even at such a liberal school, where there were classes on porn that his fellow students clamored to get into, plus parties galore if you knew where to look, Rick was aware of some things that simply couldn't be taught—at least in a lecture hall. Things like how to calm the raging erections he found himself sprouting during class when the hot girls showed up in skimpy tank tops, tossing their silky hair to the left and then the right, lifting it up and piling it on top of their heads with a barrette. Things like how to actually speak to a pretty girl, rather than just stammering stupidly. Things like how to woo two girls into his bed at once, like his buddy Kevin did; he'd seen him walking around with a blonde and a redhead, both sexy as could be, strolling the campus as if all he needed was a brunette to complete his fantasy.

There was one girl in class, Eliza, who simply mesmerized him. She wasn't necessarily the hottest girl, the one with the biggest boobs or the prettiest smile. She wasn't nearly as flashy as some of the other women he went to school with, but something about her, from her old-fashioned name to the things she wore (little cardigans decorated with flowers or sparkly bits that always caught the sun) to the way she held her pen, her fingers resting atop its length as opposed to wrapped around it like everyone else (yes, he'd noticed even that), made him want to talk to her. Okay, truth be told, he wanted to do more than simply talk. He wanted to kiss her all over, taste every inch of her beautiful skin. Most of all, he wanted to lick her pussy until she screamed. Until she came all over him. Until she went absolutely, completely, totally wild. Until she told him she'd never been with anyone who could make her climax so hard. Until she begged him to do it again.

That's what Rick thought about as Professor Vanderbilt wrote on the whiteboard and walked them through hypothetical problems they'd encounter running their own company. The only business he wanted to start, or be part of, was one that taught guys how to really eat pussy. Even thinking of those words—*eat* and *pussy*—gave him an instant hard-on. Rick shifted in his seat as his eyes swept along Eliza's back, hunched over as she doodled in her notebook. He'd lucked out with a seat near hers, but across the aisle, so that he was free to observe her unnoticed.

It wasn't that he hadn't been with girls before. Even in his sleepy small town, there'd been plenty of opportunities for sex. Marta had "made him a man," as his best friend Kyle would say, one day in a pile of leaves in a deserted park on their way home from school. Sex with her had been fun, but he'd been so nervous that he could barely enjoy it. She'd let him fuck her, but had balked when he'd asked her to spread her legs for him so he could taste her. Apparently, where she came from, nice girls didn't do that—even when they were asked by sweet boys who'd just offered up their virginity.

His only other experience with a mouthful of girl parts was with Katie, who'd pressed his face against her sex and ground herself onto him through a thin layer of panty. He'd been able to taste her unique flavor through the cotton, but it had been so brief, just a tease. He'd wanted her to relax and savor the experience, let him gently peel down her undies to reveal the treasure beneath, but she'd been so demanding, pressing and slamming and shoving against his eager-to-please tongue, that he didn't know how to tell her to slow down, nor did he ask her to remove the flimsy but still pesky panty barrier. Before he knew it, she was dragging him up by his hair, kissing his lips, pushing her wet panties aside, then guiding his cock inside her.

Rick had come to Berkeley ready to find a girl who'd want him for more than just momentary pleasures, though the idea made him nervous. A real girlfriend would expect more from him than a cursory lick and pinch of her clit. She'd want him to get down there and stay until he could prove he knew what he was doing. And even more than wanting the rapture of seeing a girl's pretty lips wrapped around his dick, like he'd seen in the porn movies that his suitemates seemed to spend an inordinate amount of time watching on their communal TV, he wanted to make a girl come with just his lips and tongue. He wanted to feel her wetness rubbing against him, taste her juices, hear her moans.

As it turned out, Eliza was the one who approached him, that very day in economics class. She stood in front of his desk as he gathered up his belongings, giving a start when he realized that the girl of his dirty dreams was right in front of him.

"Hi—Rick, right?" she asked, then licked her lips, fidgeting from one side to the other. Her hair, held back by barrettes with butterflies on them, stayed in place, but he noticed a slight bounce to her breasts. "I wanted to see if you'd like to be study partners. Vanderbilt suggested to me during office hours that I find someone and, well, I thought you might need some help in here too." She looked at him with wide, hopeful eyes, eager for his approval. He stared back, trying to see if she meant more than simply mastering means and medians and stock market prices. He wasn't sure, but his cock seemed to answer for him, surging upward in his pants.

"Yeah, that'd be great."

"What about tonight?" she asked, then looked away, as if she regretted sounding too eager.

"Tonight's fabulous," Rick told her, both because he'd get to see her sooner and because his roommate would be out until at least one in the morning at some fraternity function. He waited until they'd exchanged numbers and he'd given her his address to let his mind slip back to fantasyland, where Eliza was on her back on his bed while he held her legs apart and dove between them. His mouth watered, as if he could already taste her. He glanced up to see her walk out the door, and wondered what kind of underwear—if any—she sported beneath her tight skirt. Rick looked around and noted that he was the last student remaining in the large classroom.

When she arrived at his place later that evening, Rick thought he was ready. He'd done his best to decorate his meager apartment. He'd wanted her to notice, but she barged past him right into his bedroom.

"We can study later," she said, her body poised to give him the most advantageous view of her breasts, no longer covered in a sweater, but now in a simple white button-down top that strained against her chest. She cast him a beguiling look, and he realized she didn't have to notice a damn thing about their surroundings, as long as she was ready for him. This was more than he could've hoped for, but it felt perfect. Maybe she'd been dreaming of the same thing he had all along.

"Rick, I—" she stammered then, and he smiled. She was just as nervous as he was, and he no longer worried that she'd attack him, devour him even as he tried to devour her. She wanted him, the real him, not some fictional superhero he-man. She undressed slowly, her eyes remaining locked on his even as her fingers nimbly unbuttoned and unzipped, her movements sly and sensual, until she lay there before him, totally naked, waiting, wanting.

As Eliza lay on her back, Rick dove in. At first, he barely tasted a thing, because he was moving so fast. It was as if he was swimming, kicking his legs slightly in time to his mouth's actions, while his fingers laid her open, trying to make up for lost lessons, cram semesters into minutes as he sought her sweet spots. She didn't sit up and lecture him, pointing to where their bodies joined, to demonstrate what she wanted. No; instead Eliza, ever the English major, showed but didn't tell. She'd gently lift her hips when she wanted Rick to move lower, and hold open her hood when she wanted him to attack her clit. When he was doing something right, she'd yell and moan and bang her fists on the bed, a powerful signal. Eliza moved her hips in circles at one point, and he got it, moving his tongue in corresponding circles in the other direction.

And somewhere along the way, Rick did indeed become the cocksman—and the tonguesman—of his biggest fantasies. He earned an A+ in attention to pussy detail as he licked his wide, long, warm, soft, strong tongue from the very base of Eliza's slit all the way on up, then curled it into a point and teased her clit until she groaned. He ran his fingers all over her skin, up and down her legs, then pinching along her inner thighs, all the while getting the entire lower half of his face smeared with her juices. When his tongue was completely buried inside her, his nose smashed up against her mons, he reached up to pinch those pretty little nipples he'd seen straining against the thin bras and tank tops she kept them wrapped up in during class. He even added a finger inside her, wriggling it alongside his buried tongue.

He was a natural, and his learning curve was short and fun to ride. When she finally managed to push his head aside, they were both overwhelmed by what had passed between them. By then, he didn't even want to fuck her, but preferred to wait, instead wrapping her fingers around his cock for a few quick pumps before coming in a geyser of hot semen. Eliza fell asleep soon and Rick just looked at her naked body in repose, so lush and gorgeous, so much more than he ever could have hoped for in class.

Weeks later, again feeling bored in Professor Vanderbilt's class, he took a moment to think about Eliza's beloved pussy, the one he now got to taste every single day, often several times. No matter how his official report card turned out, he'd mastered the most important lesson of all—but that didn't mean he'd stopped trying to learn. Far from it, Rick thought, as he patted the small egg vibrator tucked in his pocket. He planned to surprise Eliza with it while he licked her to ecstasy later that night, and could practically feel the vibrations ripping through her already and hear her moans of bliss.

Letting the professor's words travel over him, he stared at Eliza's back, thought of her tasty cunt, and looked forward to earning his extra credit in Cunnilingus 101.

JOCELYN BRINGAS

SHADY WAYS

AMIE PASTOREA ROLLED HER EYES when she saw her roommate, Rina St. John, and Rina's blond boyfriend, Nick McNamara, fooling around. She couldn't believe she had to endure them for her entire freshman year. Their giggles and kissing noises were really irritating as she tried to concentrate on writing a composition for her English class.

Her anger escalating, she slammed her binder shut, grabbed her toiletries bag, and stormed out of the dorm room. Walking down the corridor, she cringed when she heard moaning from nearly every direction. She hated being in Margood Dorm, the horniest dorm on campus. Since she had enrolled late, she hadn't gotten the dorm she'd requested.

Erotic energy surrounded her. Was she the only person on campus not having sex? Still, with all the moaning she heard, she couldn't help but get aroused. She walked into the wing's bathroom, found an empty shower stall, and turned on the water to let it warm up.

Once undressed, she stepped inside the stall and relished the feeling of the hot water spraying down on her, easing her tense muscles. She lathered the soap into her hands and rubbed the bubbles all over her body, paying special attention to her nipples and the valley between her legs. As she caressed her full breasts, she threw her head back in pleasure, imagining it was Nick who was tweaking her nipples.

Even though the handsome blond was dating Rina, she couldn't help the nasty thoughts she had about him. His image flooded her mind as she slid her hand over her flat stomach, then slipped it between her legs and started to furiously rub her pulsing clit.

She let out a whimper as she imagined Nick thrusting his cock deep inside her. The familiar sensation of an orgasm struck her, and she started to grind her pussy harder onto her hand. Leaning back against the tiled shower wall, she softly moaned Nick's name as her clit seemed to burst in pleasure. She stayed in that position for a moment as she regained her breath.

Painfully removing her fingers from her clit, she stood directly under the showerhead before she turned off the water. She dried her body quickly, then slipped on her bathrobe and walked over to the sink.

The bathroom door opened and in walked Nick.

Damn coed bathrooms.

He smirked at her, and she focused her attention on the mirror. She hated him for being so handsome and having such bad taste in women. After brushing her teeth, she gathered her things and made her exit.

At least he was out of her and Rina's dorm room now. She could probably sleep in peace without having to endure the sight and sounds of Rina and Nick screwing like animals on the nearby twin bed. Her hand was on the doorknob to her room when a large hand covered it. She turned to see Nick grinning mischievously at her.

"I thought you and Rina were done for the night," she said, quickly removing her hand from under his.

"Actually, I'm here to see you. Calculus is murdering me, and I know you happen to be the math whiz. So can you help me out on the homework?"

Jamie wanted to say no and let him fail, but a nagging voice inside her head made her say yes instead.

"Cool," he grinned, "you're the best."

She returned to opening the door but he stopped her again.

"Rina's sleeping. Let's go into my dorm. My roommate's at a frat party so it'll just be us."

"Let me change first," she said, finally opening the door. After changing into her sleeping attire, she grabbed her calculus notes and quietly left the room. Nick was waiting for her.

"This way," he gestured as he started to walk. Nick was a little bit ahead of her so she had a full view of his round butt, which she had thought about numerous times. What she wouldn't give to have the opportunity to give it a nice spanking. After a few turns here and there, they arrived at his room. Walking in, she looked around and saw clutter everywhere. What irritated her most were the posters of nearly nude models plastered all over the walls.

"Excuse the mess," he said as he cleared his bed, then gestured for her to sit down. Wanting to get comfortable, Jamie sprawled out on her stomach with her notes in front of her. The bed was big enough for the two of them, so Nick lay down next to her in the same position.

"I have no freaking idea how to do problem number five," he said pointing at it in the book.

As she examined the problem, she realized she had never been this close to Nick before. After copying the problem onto her binder paper, she explained it thoroughly as Nick nodded. "Do you understand?" she asked.

"It's getting clearer," he responded.

"Good, now let me see you do number six," she said as she yawned.

"Tired?" he asked as he copied the problem onto his paper.

"Midterms are killing me."

Jamie watched as he did the problem. She noted his decent handwriting and how he concentrated deeply on the calculus problem. "I'm not sure if it's right…" he said, showing her his work. Looking at it, she smiled.

"You got it," she said handing his paper back to him. As he started the next problem, she turned onto her back. She glanced at Nick, wishing she could touch him.

"Thanks for your help," he said as he too turned onto his back and got into the same position she was in.

"Uh-huh," she said lazily, not wanting to leave the comfort of his bed.

"Don't fall asleep." He punched her arm lightly.

"I better go," she said rolling back onto her stomach. As she closed the binder, she felt a hand on her waist. She slapped it away.

"What are you doing?"

"I was touching you," he said before he pressed his lips to hers and kissed her. At first, she was in shock and didn't move. Nick kept fighting to make her kiss him back. The tip of his tongue outlined her lips and slowly her lips parted. Jamie could feel the familiar tingle of arousal between her thighs as Nick pulled her closer. She tipped her head back, and Nick's lips were all over her neck. He moved his body to cover hers. She moaned as he nibbled the side of her neck, and for a second she almost forgot he had a girlfriend. A girlfriend who was her own roommate. But once that thought crossed her mind, she pushed Nick away, making him fall down onto the cluttered floor.

"What the hell?" he muttered as he rubbed his head.

Embarrassed, she grabbed her binder and ran out. This probably had been her only chance at having him. After running away, she realized she was lost. She'd never been in this part of the dorm before. Had they walked through this common area on the way to his room? She couldn't remember. Sighing, she spotted a couch and sat down.

Tossing her binder to the side, she buried her head in her hands. She remained like that until she felt someone poking her shoulder. Lifting her head, she saw Nick, dressed only in a pair of gray sweatpants. He took a seat next to her and she accidentally glanced at his crotch.

Nick had a hard-on and it was all her fault. Still, the fact that she was the cause of it excited her. Too bad she couldn't do anything about it. They sat in silence as the murmurs of sex emanating from nearby rooms flooded their ears. Jamie wondered how people could do it all night long. It seemed like a lot of excruciating work.

"I've seen the way you look at me," he said, tracing one hand along her thigh. "And I've been watching you, too."

"What about Rina?"

"What about her?"

She couldn't remember what about Rina. Not with Nick's hand moving up her leg, higher and higher. Jamie moaned when she felt Nick's hand slide inside her pajama bottoms. Her head leaned back against the cushion as he softly massaged her through her panties. She arched her back as he rubbed her with his palm. Quickly, Nick pulled her pants and panties off her and spread her legs wide. He easily slipped two fingers inside her and started to move them in and out.

"You like that, baby?" he whispered huskily as he pumped his fingers faster. Her response was a moan as she bucked her hips wildly against him. The feelings of pleasure built up inside her and she came all over his hand, her juices soaking his fingers.

"Sweet," he said after licking her juices off his fingers. He lifted her T-shirt next, and Jamie gripped his head as his tongue tickled her nipples. Cupping a breast in each hand, he pushed them together as he swung his tongue from nipple to nipple. Nick stared at her intently as he slowly moved the tip of his tongue around one of her hardened nipples. She found that intensely erotic.

He kissed his way down her body, and then placed her legs onto his broad shoulders as he dove his lips into her pussy.

"Oh, yes," she groaned as she felt his tongue circle her drenched pussy. His hands held her hips as he lifted her up and licked her pussy. Jamie shuddered as she had another orgasm. She hadn't known a person could climax more than once in such a short amount of time.

Nick kicked out of his sweatpants before moving up next to her on the sofa and lazily nibbling her earlobe. She could feel his erection pressing against her thigh, so dangerously close to her pussy. Wrapping her arms around him, she raked her fingers down his back and right to his firm butt. She squeezed his skin and felt him grow harder.

"Damn, that feels good," he muttered.

After massaging his butt, she reached down and held his hardness. Nick was as rigid as steel when she gripped him. Precome was already making Nick's cock glow, and she could see the veins pulsing.

"That's it," he moaned as Jamie started to stroke him.

"Nick?"

"Yeah baby…"

"I want to suck your cock," she said, and she felt Nick's dick twitch in her hands. Quickly, he moved into a kneeling position, giving Jamie room to suck him.

"Yeah, suck it," he groaned, holding her head in his hands as he fucked her mouth. It took a while for her to get accustomed to his length. He was so big and thick, but she did her best, sucking him until she felt him pull away from her.

"Tell me you want me," Nick ordered as he pushed Jamie back down onto the couch. It was such a nice rush, especially being out in the open, where anyone could walk in anytime. But it was so late in the evening. What was the likelihood that they'd be caught?

"I want you, Nick," she moaned.

Nick grabbed her legs and placed them on his shoulders again, his stiff dick resting on her stomach and his balls brushing her clit.

"Please," she begged, not being able to take it anymore.

Without warning, Nick inserted his full length into her and Jamie felt like she was being split apart. She moaned and whimpered as she felt him pump into her, and she squealed when Nick lifted her up and set her with her chest pressed against his, still joined as one. His breath was coming in short gasps and his skin was bathed in sweat. He kissed her bare shoulder as he slowly moved himself inside her.

"Ride me, baby…" Nick whispered, lying back down. Pressing her palms onto his chest, she lifted her hips and slid back down. She liked the feeling of power as she rode Nick's cock. It was thrilling to have him writhing under her and grunting in pleasure.

Nick's hands were on her hips, guiding her as they moved in unison. *This is way better than masturbating!* she thought as the surges of pleasure ran all over her body. She could feel it everywhere and not just at her core. Nick leaned his head up and tried to nibble on her jiggling nipples.

"God," she groaned as he added to her pleasure. She could feel the tingly sensation of an intense orgasm approaching. Nick slammed into her so hard she could barely see what was in front of her, and she didn't protest when he flipped her around and took her doggy-style. She could only hear the slapping of skin on skin, and Nick's grunts.

Jamie felt herself drowning in a world of pleasure. Her pussy started to contract around Nick's cock, which sparked his orgasm. Nick thrust into her until he was empty. She fell facedown onto the couch as she tried to catch her breath.

"Oh, my God!" a female voice yelled.

Jamie lifted her head up for one moment and through her faltering vision she saw Rina with her eyes widened in shock. She could feel Nick scrambling to get his pants on as he hurried to run after her.

"I'm sorry, baby," Jamie heard him say to Rina as he went after her. Turning around, she grabbed her own clothing and covered up her private parts. She felt tears sting her eyes as the reality that Nick would never love her back struck her. She was just something to do while Rina was sleeping.

Jamie felt dizzy when she tried to stand up. After dressing, she walked down the hall. When she turned the corner, her heart sank as she saw Nick passionately kissing Rina. She felt disgusted, but wasn't that payment for her own shady ways?

COLLEGE REUNION

"COUNT THEM OFF," Grant growled.

I wanted to giggle, my predicament was so clichéd. But no laughter was able to bubble past my lips. It wasn't so much fear as anticipation that caused my breathing to quicken. Pressed against the hard, polished wood of the old desk, my nipples were taut and swollen. My cunt quivered, my clit throbbed, and I could smell my slick arousal.

Any moment now, the hallowed halls of my alma mater would resonate with the sound of Grant's broad palm making sharp contact with my mostly bare ass.

Hell of a college reunion!

We'd arrived that afternoon, gone to the orientation and picked up name tags, and then attended a cocktail party where we'd gotten seriously tipsy on Merlot and seriously horny about each other.

I was glad to see my college buddies, I really was. But I'd brought my husband to my ten-year reunion because I'd wanted to show him the college itself.

Culpepper University: a small, private New England school with ivy-choked walls and a hallowed central green. I adored the place, its old brick buildings with echoing, labyrinthine corridors; study rooms with fireplaces and sofas that smelled ever so faintly of dust and mildew; halls lined with portraits of former deans glowering down in disapproval at the fashions and actions of the latest generation of students.

Grant and I had been apart for a few weeks before this trip, with him working long hours at the architectural firm and me flying to Prague on short notice. So we were feeling frisky by the time we'd arrived, but we'd had no time to fool around before the planned activities started.

The cocktail party ebbed and flowed around us, and now we stood with our backs to a cavernous fireplace listening to the various conversations. No fire was lit on this early spring evening, probably because the chimney was ancient and unsafe, but the room was crowded and hot. I fanned myself with my cocktail napkin.

Grant helped, reaching up to lift my hair away from the back of my neck. I sighed as the air hit my warm flesh, then again when he tickled his fingers along my vulnerable nape.

"I don't know how much more of this I can take," he whispered, his breath against my neck making me shiver with delight. "I feel like a freshman with a major boner, and all I want to do is get some gorgeous coed back to my room and do her before I go insane."

"Just 'some gorgeous coed'?" I teased. "Any one will do?"

His hand slowly made its way down my back, curving around

my hip to stop, resting possessively on my ass. "No," he murmured. "One in particular."

"Hmm." I took a sip of wine. It was a good vintage, with an earthy hint of truffles. What I really wanted to do, right that moment, was unbutton Grant's dove-gray silk shirt and splay my hands across his warm smooth flesh, feel his heart beating beneath my palm as I tongued his dusky nipples.

Very quietly, I told him so, feeling a thrill of satisfaction when his nostrils flared as he took the image in.

"I think we—" he started to say, but then a hearty male voice broke into our private moment.

"Elise! So good to see you."

"Dr. Sherman, it's wonderful to see you, too." I introduced Grant to the handsome classics professor who'd been one of my mentors during my time at Culpepper. We chatted for a few minutes before Dr. Sherman moved on.

"I had the wickedest crush on Dr. Sherman," I admitted to Grant. "I used to fantasize about him and masturbate."

Grant's eyes widened. "*Naughty* Elise," he said. "Tell me more."

He drew me over to a window alcove. A once-scarlet velvet cushion, now faded and flattened with defeat, covered the stone seat, over which arched a tall trefoil window. When we sat, we were partially hidden by the gold brocade curtain.

"It was his voice, partially," I said, dreamily thinking back on Dr. Sherman's bass rumble, which conjured up Barry White. "And his eyes. He was so nice, yet so commanding at the same time."

"Did you ever…?"

"God, no! He was my professor! Strictly on the up-and-up."

"But you were hot for him," Grant prodded.

"Oh, yes. He fueled many of my fantasies." Grant knew I hadn't dated a lot in college. I hadn't been completely inexperienced, but I'd been something of a geek, more interested in my studies than partying, so I didn't have a lot of opportunity to get laid.

He'd helped me make up for lost time when we met in grad school.

Grant's hand was sliding up my leg as I talked, from my knee to my thigh. In another moment, he might slip it beneath my skirt, or push it up high enough to reveal to the room that I was wearing a garter belt and lace-topped stockings.

I was torn between the fear of being spotted—not that I had a huge concern about any individuals here, just the general awkwardness—and the desire that was causing my panties to dampen.

Grant leaned in and kissed me, a possessive, claiming kiss that had me pressed back against the window as his mouth plundered mine. My body sizzled with heat that had nothing to do with the room's air circulation.

It had everything to do with craving the feel of Grant's mouth and hands elsewhere on me. I wanted him to continue his way up my thigh, part my legs, and find out just how wet and needy I was.

I wanted two fingers in my cunt and his thumb on my engorged clit. It wouldn't take long to bring me to blissful release.

"Let's get out of here," Grant muttered.

"Yes."

Our wineglasses abandoned by the window seat, we grabbed our coats from the anteroom and fled before anyone could stop us to reminisce about the good ol' days.

Grant headed for the car, but I tugged at his hand and said, "This way."

The campus was deserted; the students had dispersed for the Easter holidays and the alumni were all inside getting sozzled and exchanging business cards. There wouldn't even be a wayward janitor in Kutzer Hall, the English and humanities building, our destination.

I'd spent far too much time there as a student. I'd loved the old, creaking hall, with its rabbit warren of corridors and classrooms and lounges and alcoves. Books were everywhere, crammed onto shelves that would probably collapse if you sneezed too hard.

"They never locked the building," I told Grant as we wandered the dark, echoing corridors. "I'd come here in the middle of the night to read or study, or just…I don't know. I just loved it here."

I found one of my favorite rooms, a lounge-cum-library full of moldering books and ancient brown leather sofas and paneled walls, plus a couple of massive oak desks. It was out of the way and had never been a top destination for most students. It had been a great place to study in peace.

I pulled Grant down onto one of the creaking sofas.

"One night," I said, indulging in my earlier fantasy and plucking open the top buttons of his shirt, "I was in here reading—Chaucer, I think, or maybe Shakespeare. Probably Chaucer, because I fell asleep."

"Oh, that's sexy," he said, but the thickness of his cock, pressing against his tailored pants, said otherwise.

"Yeah. Well. Something woke me up. I have no idea what time it was. They never turn off the wall lights in here." The lamps in question had been modified from gas sconces at some point. "Two, three a.m., I think. I couldn't figure out what had happened at first, but then I heard them."

"Them?"

I shivered, remembering. "The couple. They were on another sofa— that one, I think," I said, pointing. "I didn't want to look, in case they saw me. At first it was because I was embarrassed: I didn't want them to know I'd been spying. But then it was because I didn't want them to stop."

"Stop what?"

"Making out," I said. My voice was a little shaky from remembered desire. "Having sex."

"Tell me," Grant said.

The commanding tone in his voice made me shiver again, deliciously. His hand covered my breast, making slow, lazy circles, and even through the thin raspberry cashmere and my lace bra, my nipple responded, pushing back against his palm.

"Even though I couldn't see them, I could tell by the noises what they were doing. In some ways it was even hotter, just listening to them, imagining. They were kissing, and I could hear soft, wet sounds. Then he did something and she gasped. She sounded startled, but really aroused, too. I think he might have been giving her a hickey."

"Like this?" Grant lowered his mouth to my neck. His teeth scraped across my flesh, biting just hard enough to elicit a flash of pleasurable pain.

"Oh God, yes." I let my head fall back against the sofa so he'd have easy access to plunder my flesh from ear to collarbone.

"Go on," he said.

"He kept telling her how beautiful she was, how sexy. I couldn't decide if he was just buttering her up or if he meant it, but I think he did. He sounded almost…*astonished.* Grateful.

"They moved around a little, and then she murmured something like 'yes, oh yes.' I'm pretty sure she'd taken off her shirt and he was playing with her breasts."

"Mm." Both of Grant's hands insinuated themselves beneath my sweater, and his thumbs stroked across my aching nipples. Unbidden, I arched my back, pushing toward the sensation. He rolled my peaks between his fingers, and I felt it all the way down to my clit.

He told me to keep talking, and I did.

"Remember 'Paradise By the Dashboard Light'? It was like that. They were breathing hard, whimpering, and they got to the point when anything they said was in short gasps, like they were just completely unable to get out full sentences.

"They readjusted again, or shifted, or something, and from the wet sloppy noises I figured out she was giving him a blow job. I peeked out then, and I could see the top of his head against the back of the sofa, so she must have been on her knees in front of him. I imagined he had his hands on her head, not forcing her, but just encouraging her. She laughed at one point; this low, husky laugh; and asked him if he liked that. All he could do was moan."

"Did she bring him off?" Grant sounded a little strained himself, probably because I was massaging the thick length of his cock through his pants. I reached for his belt, but he stayed my hand. He wanted me to keep talking, getting off on the story as much as I was.

"Not yet. By that point I was so horny myself from listening to them that I could hardly stand it. It felt like it took me five minutes just to unzip my jeans, because I was moving so slowly to keep them from hearing anything. My panties were soaked—oh God!"

Grant had decided to check whether my panties were soaked now, and the feel of his fingertips grazing across my crotch brought my hips off the sofa. He brought his fingers to his lips, tasting me. Yes, my panties were wet through and through.

He reached back down and slowly stroked me, still over the panties, while I struggled to keep a straight thought in my head and continue the story. I told him how I'd forced my hand down into my jeans, under my panties, pinching my nipple with my other hand. "I could hear the anonymous couple shift position yet again, and when she squealed, I knew he'd pushed his cock into her."

"They got a little louder at that point. His breath rasped and she couldn't stop whimpering incoherently. His hips slapped against her ass, faster and faster, until suddenly he stopped. I held my breath, and she probably held hers, too, before the sofa creaked under the sudden, arrhythmic flurry of his thrusts as he came.

"I stuffed my fist in my mouth to keep myself from screaming as I came, too. Thankfully, it didn't take long for them to pull themselves together and leave. I pulled my hand out of my pants and licked my wet fingers clean."

Grant's cock twitched when I admitted that part. I was so close to coming myself, from telling him the details of the dirty story and the memory of how hard I'd come from listening to the anonymous couple and the feel of his fingers teasing my clit, not quite hard enough.

"Come here."

Grant was tugging me to my feet. Drugged with arousal, I complied.

He pulled his long-abandoned tie out of his pocket as we walked over to one of the old oak desks. Confused, I still didn't figure out what was up until he was wrapping the silk around my wrists and gently pressing a hand between my shoulder blades to encourage me to bend over.

"Grant!" We'd played with bondage and spanking before, but I hadn't expected it right now. I figured we'd fuck on the sofa and be done (at least for a few hours).

A tremor, like a mini-orgasm, rocked through me when he tied the other end to a drawer handle. My upper body was flat against the desktop. My feet barely touched the floor, just enough to keep my balance.

My ass was entirely vulnerable.

He pushed my skirt up to my hips. My white lace boy-shorts would do nothing to protect my vulnerable cheeks from his onslaught.

The first smack is always the worst. No matter how hard I tried to relax, my buttcheeks were clenched, and I felt the sting spread. The second spank came quickly, as did the third, alternating.

Four, five, not in any order or speed. I could imagine my reddening flesh was visible through the lace.

I needed to come so badly. The blows reverberated down to my clit. Six, seven, eight. My nipples, my pussy, my ass…my entire body felt like one huge sexual organ.

Nine. Heat, everywhere.

Ten.

Cool air rushed against my burning ass and steaming cunt as Grant yanked the panties down my legs and off one foot. I spread my legs as best I could.

I knew he was as desperate as I was. It was my only saving grace—if he'd teased me now, I would have dissolved in anguish.

His belt buckle jingled as he dropped his pants, and a moment later, he slid straight into me with no resistance.

It took only a few strokes before my inner muscles clenched and pulsed around him and I screamed, not caring how the sound reverberated in the empty room. I felt like my whole body convulsed in orgasm.

It took a moment for both of us to recover. Finally Grant kissed the back of my neck and pulled out of me. I heard him pull up his pants.

"You okay?" he asked.

"Fantastic," I purred.

His come trickled down my inner thighs. Oh, how I must look, stretched across the desk, ass red, clearly and soundly fucked.

Grant didn't move to untie me.

"Honey?" I said.

"We're not through yet."

He reached under me and put two fingers against my clit. I was still horny, still needy, and I knew I had another major orgasm in me. I sighed with anticipatory pleasure.

Then he picked up a ruler.

My stomach lurched. Falling against my already spanked, come-flushed bottom, the strokes were going to hurt like hell.

And I knew he'd keep me on edge, wouldn't bring me off until the final blow fell.

"Count them off," Grant growled again….

Janelle's Spankology 101

OMPOSITION ASSIGNMENT 1: Letter of Goals for the School Year
Professor Hadly,
You asked us, for our first paper of the semester, to write a letter about what we want to get out of the school year. I want to get the most out of each class that is possible. I want to keep myself on the path that will lead to a successful career.

I want…

I want to fuck my roommate's boyfriend until I can't walk to your class tomorrow, after I spank him like my roommate is doing RIGHT NOW.

Shit! I hurriedly deleted that last bit before I accidentally kept it as part of my paper. Then I gave up working on the assignment, since I wasn't able to concentrate anyway. Turning from my monitor to the couple across the room, I tamped down the stirrings of jealousy I was feeling.

Watching my roommate with her lover bent over her lap, spanking his bare ass with a hairbrush, I barely resisted the urge to slide a hand down my pants and finger my clit. Ever since the night I had come home early from work to find him tied to her desk chair and Janelle spread out naked before him on her desk like the redhead buffet that he was feasting on, they had stopped hiding their bedroom antics. As if nothing was happening, I had nonchalantly settled myself into bed and tried to sleep.

After that, Janelle knew I could handle their relationship, and that was enough for her. I guess it never entered her mind that despite being okay with it, I was also turned on by their exhibitionism, and a bit jealous, too. Hearing the not-so-subtle sounds of Janelle and Terence screwing in the dark was a lot different than watching her slender hand land blow after blow across his ass with a hairbrush.

I wished I could find a guy willing to take a spanking from me, but it just never worked out. Most of the guys I dated long enough to confess a desire to spank had simply humored me, expecting a few light smacks. As for the others, they couldn't get past my diminutive height long enough to let me control anything.

Janelle landed a particularly hard blow, and I couldn't help but wince as Terence moaned. Maybe there was something to be said for dating a jock, after all. Janelle delivered another hard smack, and this time it was me who moaned as his rich chocolate-colored ass lifted, silently begging for more. Oh, how I wanted to give it to him, too!

I couldn't help the muffled groan that escaped my mouth at my vision of Terence's smooth, dark butt raised in supplication while I smacked my bare hand against it. The mental image was enough to send shivers down my spine.

"You okay?" Janelle asked. Since Terence was sporting a big, red, brand-new ball gag, I figured the question was for me.

"Fine, although I think maybe I should leave you two alone." I wanted to be snide and add, *Since I'm not able to get any studying done anyway,* but that would come off as me being a jealous bitch. After sharing my bedroom at home with three younger sisters, I could handle the background noise, if only it weren't so tantalizing.

If only my parents knew just what I was learning in college!

A soft yelp drew my attention back to the couple across the room. Since the sound couldn't have come from the gagged football player, I couldn't help but wonder what he had done to make Janelle yelp.

"Angela, come here a minute." Sighing softly, and hoping like hell she wouldn't be able to smell my arousal, I got up and crossed the tiny room. Although I had seen Janelle changing clothes and thus completely naked before, her bare breasts with their caramel nipples still drew my attention. She was definitely cheerleader material, with her pixie face, almost perfect body, and mile-long legs. Still, given how good she looked in a leather corset, I was tempted to start a campaign to change their uniform from cotton to leather. Janelle gave Terence's shoulder a gentle nudge and he moved back, kneeling beside her chair. Pointing at the bed, she quietly demanded that he lie across it. When he moved to comply, her steady gaze then turned to me. I could easily have drowned in her green eyes, they were so full of life and fire. Her very personality and zest shined brightly through, no matter what she was doing.

And I knew the picture I presented to her: tousled wet hair, thanks to my morning swim routine; milky white face bare of makeup; baggy khaki pants; and an even baggier T-shirt. Next to her perfect hair and makeup, I was a train wreck.

She held up the hairbrush and offered it to me, handle first. "Give him a good one."

I tried to laugh, but nothing came out. She couldn't be serious. This was her *boyfriend,* and while spanking him in front of me was one thing, this was totally different.

"Go on." She pressed the hairbrush into my palm, forcing me to take it. Standing up, she moved around behind me, her breasts brushing against the thin material covering my back. Braless, there was nothing between her and me except well-worn cotton.

"Janelle, I…"

Her hands settled on my hips, coaxing me forward, toward Terence's deliciously raised ass.

"Go on."

I stepped closer and raised the brush. I swung downward, the brush landing with a soft smack.

"No, no, no. Harder." Her hand settled over mine and together we swung. *SMACK!*

"Yes! That's it, Angela. Again."

Palm sweating, I tightened my grip and swung again. The brush landed against his flesh with a loud crack. My pussy clenched. My head swam as I watched Terence jerk forward then arch back again, silently begging for more. And I wanted to give more to him. So I did. *SMACK!*

Spanking him felt so good. Janelle pressed tighter against me, moving with every twitch I made. I smacked him again, and watched his asshole pucker.

The rush was absolutely amazing. I was hot, needy, and loving every tiny tremor that wracked Terence's body. He wanted it, craved what I was giving to him, and I needed to give it to him.

I was so wrapped up in what I was doing that I almost forgot Janelle, until I felt her slowly lifting my T-shirt.

"What…" I began to ask, but she cut me off, pressing a manicured fingertip against my lips.

"Just relax. Spank him again."

Her cool hands slid around my rib cage, brushing lightly over my skin, her movements unthreatening. I could feel the hard pebbles of her nipples against my back with each breath she took.

Looking back to Terence's ass, I couldn't resist. I smacked him again, and again. Fingertips moved up to my breast, tweaking my nipples with each swing. I was drugged by the sweet euphoria. His ass, so rich, sweet, and dark, lifting to each punishing blow I landed against it.

My pussy quivered, and instinctively I answered its call. Slipping a hand under the waistband of my khakis, I slid them down until the cloth brushed against my clit. Circling the tiny bud, I worked myself into a frenzy of erotic motion.

Janelle's hands were just as busy, her long fingernails pinching my nipples, sending tingles of pain straight to my pussy.

I was almost there, tiny tremors heralding the wave to come. I was ready to slide to the floor, a pool of Jell-O. Just one more, I needed just one more.

SMACK!

I tossed the brush on the bed, closed my eyes, and leaned back into Janelle's touch, letting her pinch and play with my nipples, her lips pressing soft kisses against my neck and ear as I slid my other hand into my pants, thrusting two fingers into my cunt.

Oh sweet God, I needed this.

My pussy clenched around my fingers, juices already coating them. Thrusting in and out, I knew my pants tented obscenely in the front but I didn't care.

At some point after I tossed the brush aside, Terence must have rolled over, because when I opened my eyes I met his knowing look. Deep, dark brown, his eyes were almost mesmerizing for the sensual knowledge they held.

Trailing my gaze down his body, I couldn't help but admire his firm contours. Not only had football toughened him up, but he also had the appearance of someone who swam and ran track. Where most serious football players had bulging muscles, his were sleeker, more defined.

I wanted him. I wanted his cock between my legs, not my own fingers. I wanted to ride his cock until I exploded, and then spank his ass while he jerked himself off. I wanted to tie him up, shove the hairbrush handle up his ass, and suck him off.

Just thinking about his cock drew my gaze further down. There it was, thick, solid, rich chocolate, just waiting to be devoured. His cockhead had an angry red tint, as if he was ready to come, but was unable to.

Janelle must have sensed my interest, for after biting my earlobe gently she whispered, "He can't come 'til I let him. See that slender strip at the base of his cock? It's called a cock ring."

I trembled with the knowledge. Two orgasms, five orgasms, ten. It didn't matter. I could ride him all day without him leaving me behind.

Janelle's hands left my breasts and gripped my pants. With a not-so-gentle tug, she pooled them at my ankles.

"Go ahead, Angela. Climb on."

I hesitated, earning me a bare-handed swat across the ass.

"I said, go ahead."

Pulling my soaked fingers from my cunt, I wrapped them around his cock. He felt so hard, so thick. And my pussy craved him.

Without giving myself time to second-guess and doubt the moment, I straddled him. Leaning forward, I slid down onto his cock, taking him within me an inch at a time.

I felt full, stretched, once he was fully inside me, my ass settling onto his thighs.

Janelle pressed a hand to my neck, pushing me to lie flush against him, when all I wanted to do was be cowgirl to his pony and ride him off into the sunset.

"Please," I whimpered. But Janelle held me pressed down. Terence's arms wrapped around my shoulders, holding me tight against his chest.

I heard the air swish, then the smacking sound of hairbrush against flesh. How had she hit him, when I was on top of him?

Then I felt it, the fire spreading through my ass. I yelped.

Again she smacked me, and I wailed her name, struggling in Terence's grip. But he held me tight. My five-foot frame didn't stand a chance against his huge, muscular body.

I knew that if I just said no they would let me go, but I couldn't.

Again she smacked me, and the fire spread, rushing through my ass and into my cunt.

I clenched around Terence's cock and he jerked, his chest hair brushing my nipples. She smacked me again, and the chain reaction continued.

I was helpless. I was exhilarated. The high I had felt earlier returned, mixing with the loss of control I was feeling. It was everything and nothing, rolled into one.

And again. I was in charge; I could stop this at any moment. Until then, I was helpless, completely at their mercy.

I loved the sensations rushing through me. I gave myself up to the sweet sting and rode the wave.

I lost track of the count at ten. My pussy demanded attention. Clenching tight with each pleasurable sting, I lost myself in the sensation, until with a muffled scream I came, gripping Terence's cock deep within me, allowing my roommate of two years to paddle my tender ass.

I kept my face buried in his chest, gasping for air as the world tried to right itself. If it was only one heartbeat later that I rolled to the side, or an hour, I really don't know.

With a knowing smile Janelle climbed onto the bed and took my place straddling Terence. I sat up, pressed a soft closed-mouth kiss against her lips, and whispered, "Thank you."

"Anytime Angela. Anytime."

I nodded to show I understood and turned away, giving them privacy once more. Picking up my pants, I pulled them on and sat back down at the computer to try to work on my English paper.

Behind me, I could hear Janelle removing the ball gag and cock ring. "Now baby, since you've been so good."

The sound of Terence's moan as Janelle sank down onto his cock was the sweetest sound I had ever heard.

The bed groaned and creaked as she rode him the way I had fantasized about, like I knew I would myself one day.

Turning my attention to my screen and trying my best to ignore the steady throbbing sting of my ass, I started typing.

Composition Assignment 1: Letter of Goals for the School Year

Professor Hadly,

You asked us, for our first paper of the semester, to write a letter about what we want to get out of the school year.

What I want most is a well-rounded education. I want to know more than books can tell me, although I do want that knowledge as well.

I want to leave college feeling as if I truly got the most out of it. Up until now, I have been settling for book knowledge, immersing myself within the pages, until I have no room left for anything else. But that ends now. I want to learn what books can't teach us. What no one has been able to put into words yet.

I guess I just want it all, and I'm not going to settle anymore for anything less.

Life demands sacrifices and risks, to truly be lived. And I am ready to start living.

JOEL A. NICHOLS

I WANTED HIM TO FEEL IT

CORNER OF CHURCH AND HIGH. Is your house closer?"

"Yes," I said and kissed him hard. It was his first time kissing a boy and I wanted him to feel it. He pulled back, put one hand on the nape of my neck, and reached for his cigarettes with the other. I still had two fingers just inside the top of his waistband when he asked me where I lived.

I led him away from the party, two blocks uphill and into my house.

When we got there he smoked another cigarette, and I lay down on the carpet in front of him, waiting with my hands behind my head. "What are you doing down there?" he said, and started to unbutton his shirt.

I wondered if all straight guys talked dumb like that as he crawled on top of me, digging his sharp hips into mine. We started kissing again, hard. Rougher than I'd expected—almost as hard as I'd tried to the first time, back at the party.

I moved one hand under his shirt and the other to his ass. He helped me pull off his shirt and I saw skinny silver rings curving through both nipples. I went for them immediately, sucking hard with the tip of my tongue and the edges of my teeth. "Careful," he breathed out, "I just did them." I pushed against them with my tongue and he fumbled at my belt.

I moved to help him with the clasp, but wanted to see if he could get my pants open on his own. They were my favorite pants that semester: tattered brown corduroys that made my legs look skinny and my crotch huge. A few seconds later he yanked at my waist and ripped out the rivet, pulling the zipper down and open. I unbuttoned his pants and felt his dick getting hard.

"Let's get on the bed," I said, and by the time we made it across the two feet of cheap gray carpet, we were both nearly naked. With his plain-Jane checked boxers bunched at his ankles, he leaned back and asked me what I was into. I crawled on top of him and kissed his neck.

"Everything. What do *you* want to do?" I couldn't believe I was offering prefab dialogue worse than some lowbrow fuck movie, but I knew it would pay off with him. Shivering from too many drinks and too many cigarettes, he cast down his eyes. He was too shy to ask me to go down on him, so I went for his cock and sucked it. Matching his thin legs and meager trunk, his dick stayed slender as it got harder and filled my mouth. His balls hung low and loose, and I grabbed them. My own cock surged forward when I thought of him tasting it—the first time he would have had a cock in his mouth.

I continued to jack him off slowly and tightly, and kissed back up toward his nipples. Then I laid my head at the top of my bed, next to his. "I want you to suck me," I mumbled, and he threw his head down to my crotch. He was clumsy and rough, licking the head of my cock for a while, and then trying to swallow it. Over and over again he took almost the whole thing in and out of the back of his throat. His lips pursed around my dickhead, I finally put one hand on his head and started to guide his motions.

He was concentrating hard on my dick and I pulled a little at his curls, signaling for him to let up and head for my balls. Instead, he sucked harder and swung his body around, planting his knees on either side of my head. Within seconds, his dick was back in my mouth and I had both hands on his ass, rubbing my thumbs over the spot that is not quite ass and not quite thigh. He moved his ass against my hands and sucked harder. He had gotten better and realized it, sucking the tip of my cock, then swirling his tongue around it, up and down. The way his hips bounced, I had a hard time keeping his dick in my mouth, so I started to jack him off and lick his balls. He pushed his ass even closer to me and I started to play with his cheeks again, cautiously getting closer and closer to his asshole.

With one of his balls in my mouth, I touched the tip of my index finger to his hole and stroked a small circle. He sighed and started to jerk my dick backhanded. My dick was sopping with his spit. He pulled firmly and kept the head wet with flicks of his tongue as I started fingering him. He sighed again and began moaning. I spit on my finger and pushed in further. He pressed against my hand, taking in more of my finger. I kept my left hand around his balls and, with my right index finger buried in his ass, pumped my arm back and forth. He let go of my dick entirely and laid his sweaty head on my leg. His hands dug under the backs of my thighs while I finger-fucked him. I tried another finger and he moaned, pushed back on my hand, then pulled away from me entirely and said, "I've got a condom, in my wallet."

I had no idea which lump of black shadows on my floor was his pants, and reached down beside the bed for one of my own. I groped for a packet of lube I knew was mixed in with the condoms. He lay on his back while I tore open the package and rolled it down myself. I went down on him again, took his dick in my mouth, and put two spit-and-lube-wet fingers up his ass. He pressed himself against my fingers again, then moved his hips and starting saying, "Please." I took my hand away and lifted his legs in the air. Guiding the head of my dick with my right hand, I found his ass and eased in. He gasped as I slid in and I held it there for a second, then went deeper. It was too much for him and he pulled away. I thought for a second I'd lost him by rushing it, but he turned over and climbed up on his knees.

In that position my cock slid right in, and I started fucking him doggy-style, one of my hands reaching toward his shoulder and one planted on his hip. I pumped slow at first to let him adjust, but he started meeting my thrusts, throwing his ass against my cock faster and faster, pulling my dick deep into him. His ass held my cock firm in all directions. He was so tight I had to start holding off immediately. I leaned back and took both of his hips in my hands, guiding his thrusts as he slammed hard onto my cock.

He moaned, softly at first, like when I was fingering him, and then louder and louder. I was sure he was about to wake up my roommate, asleep in the next room, and was wondering if we should change positions when his ass tightened and breathlessly I started to come—I just couldn't stop. I arched over him, my chest covering his sweat-slicked back, and thrust until we were both finished. Then I pulled out and rolled us both over as I palmed the condom and dropped it to the floor. My dick dragged wet over his thigh and I kissed him, soft and slow.

It was his first time with a boy, and I wanted him to feel it.

,

SAVANNAH STEPHENS SMITH

Call Me Jenny

ALL ME JENNY—"

"Yes, Mrs. D—I mean, Jenny."

The denim was soft, but underneath was steely. Hard. The erection only achieved by men still under twenty-five. To me, they're boys, not men, but the way he wanted me wasn't boyish. Not in the least.

We sat in my driveway in the suburbs after a long winter journey. Brent was my son's friend, and he'd given me a ride home after we'd run into each other at the international airport in the city. The last flight of my trip home was canceled because of bad weather, and Brent was at the airport, too, dropping off his roommate before heading back to his—and my—hometown. Brent's friend's flight had left, but mine hadn't. It was funny, running into him at Domestic Departures, a familiar face in a crowd of disgruntled strangers who all wanted to get home for the holidays. Instead of leaving me to wait for the next flight, Brent offered to take me with him. The snowy weather didn't deter him from a seven-hour drive—that's the way the young are.

Something made me accept his invitation. Maybe I didn't want to face a night alone in a hotel in the city where my ex-husband and his new and much younger wife lived. Maybe I just wanted to get home, the sooner the better. At any rate, I said yes. Brent fetched my luggage and we left the airport together. The last leg of my journey home would be with my son's childhood best friend. Odd, but it was better than traveling alone, and we'd known each other for years. It would be a nice chance to catch up on what he'd been doing since he graduated from university in the spring.

We'd driven through the winter day, afternoon quickly becoming evening as we left the city behind and began to weave through the mountains. Owing to the winter conditions, we traveled more slowly than if it had been summertime. I was glad Brent handled his car with caution, and I wondered if my son would be so mature. Somehow, I doubted it.

As we moved onward through the night, Brent updated me on recent events in his life. He'd started a job as an accountant with a large firm in the city, and he'd broken up with his girlfriend. He had moved into an apartment downtown with another friend from university and was enjoying the big city life. Of course he was: Brent was young, good-looking, with a bright future. Single, too. He didn't need to ask about Robbie—we both knew my son's prospects were less promising. Robbie had dropped out of school the previous year and was now attempting to beat the very long odds in the music biz. Working at minimum-wage jobs behind the counter at a CD store and behind the bar at clubs supplemented his income. If other things also supplemented his income, I didn't want to know. I could only hope his father would be able to keep Robbie in line, but I doubted that too.

Being in a car together lent the two of us an unexpected intimacy. As if under the spell of the snow falling in the headlights, the black and white night, and the cautious speed of travel, our talk turned quite frank a few hours into the journey. We discussed life and learning, love and sex. I couldn't believe the boy I'd seen grow up was now a man, but he was. Dark haired, muscular, with nice, even features. From what I could tell, he hadn't picked up the trend of tattooing and piercing whatever body part happened to be sticking out at any given time. As the trip progressed, the feeling of intimacy intensified. We were relaxed with each other now, and I felt as if we were friends, not an older woman and a young man. I suppose I flirted with Brent more than I should have, surprised to find myself enjoying his discomfort— and his arousal. I suspected he'd become erect when we'd talked about sex, because he shifted uncomfortably in the driver's seat. More than once I saw his hand automatically go down to adjust himself before he halted the gesture. I teased him, enjoying his blushes and brushes with confession. By the time we arrived at the lights of town, I'd let the situation go too far, though, and I figured he was stiff as a plank. And by the time we reached my neighborhood he wasn't the only one itching for a little sheet-slipping.

By then I was wet and acutely aware of how sometimes life could be drab without a husband—without a man, anyway. I'd been squeezing my thighs together for the past hour, aching for relief. Home. A bottle of wine, the hot tub, and my vibrator. Suddenly what had seemed so delightful when I was stuck at the airport on the coast now seemed dismal. The glamorous life of a single woman over forty. Hell, at this rate, I wouldn't even need the vibrator. A glass of wine and the hot tub jets would probably give me an orgasm. An orgasm for one. It seemed so bleak.

When Brent turned the engine off in my driveway, I leaned over and touched him, and he froze. Shock, embarrassment—enjoyment? But he didn't push my hand away, and he didn't protest. I stroked his hard-on through his jeans, fascinated, as he squirmed beneath my touch. Clearly, he'd gotten quite aroused by our talk. I bet he'd come in his jeans if I kept it up. I didn't want that. Not while I needed it more than his Levi's did.

"Come into the house, Brent," I murmured. "You need something to keep you up." He still had a way to go, now that his parents no longer lived three doors down from me. "A cup of coffee. Or…" Me, of course.

It wasn't nice to tease him, but the agony in his eyes was matched by desire. I knew that I looked good, and that this young man wanted me. And it wasn't all teasing—I needed some relief, too. Winter's cold. I was hot. And life's short.

We slogged inside, shaking snow from our shoes and shivering at the chill of an empty house. In the kitchen, I stopped pretending. Maybe it was looking around at the same old "dream kitchen" where I'd spent far too much time, the dream worn thin long ago, or maybe it was knowing my husband was never coming back, but I dropped the notion that I was going to make Brent some coffee before he continued on his journey. I had a much better way to thank him.

Impulsively, I dropped to my knees in front of him, probably frightening him. But he'd followed me into the house, hadn't he? He was a gorgeous young thing. And his parents had raised him well— even with an impressive erection, the outlines of which I could clearly see, he struggled to remain polite.

"Mrs. Douglas?" he whispered, but I had difficulty believing he was that nervous. He was twenty-two, for heaven's sake. They're nurtured on R-rated movies, must-see-TV, and trash-talking music these days, and I knew he'd had girlfriends all through high school and university. He and Robbie had been friends for years.

"Yes, Brent," I cooed, drawn to that tantalizing bulge. I couldn't remember the last time I'd seen an erection that hard in real life, and I couldn't help but stroke him more. My daring made my stomach flutter and my pussy quiver. A warm, wanting sensation urged me on. His thighs were just fine, too. And did I mention his ass? Oh, my. Soccer? Running? What sport had sculpted him? It should be mandatory for all males to partake of whatever made him so…healthy.

"What are you doing, Mrs. Douglas?"

"Call me Jenny. Honey, that thing looks like it's going to rip right through those jeans," I purred, fully aware I was acting out every cliché I'd come across from mainstream romance to triple-X-rated videos. How often do you get a chance to do it in real life? I had the chance to live out one of those afternoon fantasies, and I was going to take it. After all, it wasn't like he was unwilling. His erection said "ready, willing, and totally able."

"You don't want to show up at your house sporting this," I said, rubbing his hard-on. The genie was going to be out of the jeans soon. I desperately wanted it inside me. The ache intensified.

"No, ma'am. My mother would…"

"Yep."

A rueful chuckle from us both, because we both knew what his mother was like. Prissy, perfect Patricia. I never liked her, and she felt the same way, despite our sons' friendship. I didn't want to think about that, though.

"I bet if I were you—" I started, itching to undo the copper snap of his jeans and tug the zipper down. Brent looked like he was blessed with about seven—maybe even a smidge more—inches. Thick, too. I couldn't believe I was licking my lips, but I did. I wanted him, the urge sharp, strong, and beyond denying. "—I'd probably pull over as soon as I was out of sight of this house, and I'd have that thing out…is it as big as it looks? Never mind. I'll…" *Find out,* I thought, but didn't say it. I didn't want to scare him. "And finish myself off in, what? One, two, three strokes, tops?"

Brent was breathing pretty hard by then, standing there in front of me, but he hadn't bolted. Not yet. The nice hard-on was beginning to look a little painful, in fact, and I could make out the shape and get a good idea of the generous size of the thing. I guess the way I kept touching him as I talked wasn't helping matters much, either. "Mrs. Douglas," he muttered.

"Honey, why don't we take care of that thing in a much better way?" I squeezed, and he groaned. "Do an old lady a favor."

"You're not old," he protested, still polite.

I got up. "You're very kind."

"You're very pretty," he added, shy as a suitor.

"I'm very horny, Brent," I said, and kissed him. Hard. It was the wrong thing to do. But he was kissing me back in under a second with no time to change our minds. Then his tongue was thrusting in my mouth, hot and eager, if a little unskilled. I liked it. We kissed, surrendering to impulse.

In a minute, I pulled back. I couldn't believe I was trying to seduce him. But my body craved it, and I wanted him so badly. I was already breathing heavily and aching to rip off my sweater. I was wet. And so very bad. Life is so short, though.

If I had thought about it for more than an instant, I'd… This time, though, Brent kissed me, my eyes closing, yielding to want. I forgot who he was and only felt how he was: hard and eager, solid and strong, young and healthy. He pulled me close and I swayed against his crotch, rubbing myself against that tantalizing bulge. I'd felt plumber's pipes with more give than that. I wanted it. He backed me into the tiled countertop and ground his pelvis against mine, sucking my tongue desperately. What he lacked in technique, he made up for in intensity and enthusiasm. I didn't mind—it excited me all the more. We stopped kissing only long enough for me to pull my sweater over my head and fling it to the floor. I was wearing a plain white T beneath it, and my favorite jeans. They were three sizes smaller than I'd worn as Stanley's wife. I was my own woman now. I could do what—or whom—I wanted. All woman, all curves and desire.

I tilted my head and sought Brent's mouth again. Both of us were hungry, appetites raging in the silence of the house where he'd visited often as a boy. Now, he'd entered the house as a man. I found his hands and brought them to my breasts, and he groaned and squeezed. My nipples poked against the cotton, and I couldn't wait for him to touch them. They were aware and sensitive. I wanted touch: hand or mouth, I didn't care which. Oh, mouth, I thought, teasing his tongue with mine. Brent smelled great. He was taller than me. He probably outweighed me by fifty pounds. When had that happened? I felt dizzy.

He wore a navy polo shirt under his jacket, and I tugged it out of his jeans as we kissed, frantic to touch his skin. His back was smooth and warm beneath my fingers, broad and strong. I thumbed the belt loop of his jeans, pulled him to me, and cupped his ass. I heard myself moan. I was damp; I could feel it against my panties. I hugged him harder, my legs spread, working against his erection, already making the motions of intercourse. Denim to denim. Want to want. Age was meaningless. Blood and desire overrode everything.

I pulled his shirt out, sliding my hand up his belly, flat and hard, and found his chest. Warm and muscular, he was beautifully made. Beautifully male. I longed to nip at his skin, to flick his nipples, kiss my way down…

We stopped kissing long enough for him to yank his jacket off. It joined my sweater on the floor. I pulled my T up and his hands were on my breasts, with only the bra between his hand and my skin. I hissed with pleasure as he seized me. My nipples were throbbing hard bits that demanded touch. I wanted to rip my bra off. Instead, we kissed some more. It looked like Brent wasn't in any hurry to get to his folks' house now.

I pulled the T all the way off, wriggled out of the bra, and set my breasts free. Brent groaned, and his hands sought them, caressing my bare skin. He nuzzled me, moving from one mound to the other, in a fever to taste and touch. I touched him, too, reveling in being explored.

His hair was soft, but his mouth was driving me crazy. When he finally took one firm nipple between his lips, I made a sound like a cat. He paused, but my groan of pleasure told him to continue. He sucked my nipples as I stroked his hair and his shoulders. His mouth was hungry on my breasts, and the more he sucked, the wetter I got. His mouth and hands sent hot pangs of desire all through me, ending in my clit and deep inside my pussy.

Hours of being pleasantly horny during the drive had culminated in desire that would not be satisfied by anything less than fucking. Hard fucking. Brent's mouth was like fire on my nipples, exactly what I'd been craving as we drove, appetite building with each mile. I had been covertly touching myself as we traveled through the snowy night and talked dangerously about subjects that decorum said we should avoid. I had been confident that the darkness hid my actions. Now, what I'd imagined was happening and it was bliss, sending me into deeper yearning.

At last, impatience drove me. I needed more, needed to feel his naked body, his skin against mine. I wanted to undress him, to discover him, to finally see what he looked like naked. Brent sucked one proud nipple, his tongue rasping over the tip and making me writhe with longing. I wriggled my jeans down my hips, aching, wondering for a millisecond if he could smell it on me. Probably. I didn't care. *I'm a bitch in heat,* I thought, and palmed his pecs like he did my tits. Brent lifted his head from my skin, and we kissed. His mouth was warm, his lips soft, but his tongue was wonderfully lewd. Would he touch me? My pussy? I wriggled and squirmed, pressing my breasts against his shirt, standing there with my jeans pulled down. Never had I felt so wicked.

Brent groped between my opened legs and I moved against his hand, clutching his shoulders. Palm and fingers moved against me. I groaned when his finger sank into my wetness. He stroked me, finding my nipple again, and I swayed against his fingers. I could almost, but not quite, climax from the touch of his still-novice, half-hesitant hand alone. But it wouldn't feel as good as it would to come, tight around his cock, climaxing with that singular feeling of being filled.

I slid against one crooked finger, dancing on the edge of orgasm, and then drew back. *Fuck me,* I thought, but didn't say it, certain the spell would be broken if I voiced what we were doing. It all seemed like a dream, a housewife's three-in-the-afternoon fantasy. Soap stars and neighborhood boys fuelling desires that men like my husband had left burning, unquenched. I stood, breathing hard, stroking his taut belly, then moved my hand down to palm his cock. I pressed hard, and he made a sound.

"You must be uncomfortable," I said, and I finally got to work that brass button open. Unzipping him was a challenge, given how stiff he was, but I managed. Want finds a way. Sliding the zipper down over the length of his erection and hearing his rough breathing only excited me more. The zipper slowly went up and over the rigid bulge of his cock as I slid it open. His underwear was the only thing between what I wanted and me. I worked his prick out, crossing some boundary. It was an action I could never undo.

His cock was beautiful. It was all I'd idly dreamed of as we drove, simmering with longing: erect, warm and throbbing, nicely hefty. Brent groaned as I squeezed him, entranced by my prize and the shock of seeing his prick, real and urgent. No fantasy. Mine. Then I was on my knees before him in the clear light of the kitchen, kneeling on the oak floor. I clasped him, squeezed again, anticipating. I hadn't had anything that looked this appetizing in my kitchen for a long time. Brent's cock was nicely shaped, thick enough to make my brows fly upward, and a healthy shade of pink. He was circumcised. Even as I knew I was being one very naughty lady, I loved the way I felt in the midst of this. Brazen, bold, and bad. My jeans pulled down, my breasts bared and nipples swollen, I was completely lost to lust, high on sinning. "I'm so wet," I confessed—or bragged—stroking the silky length of him, a clear drop collecting at the swollen tip. He was helpless against it. His prick was such a pretty thing, too, and I couldn't wait to—

I leaned in and slipped the swollen, velvety head of him between my lips. A shudder went though me as my tongue met his skin. Brent cried out a half-hearted protest. He was tender and warm and I circled the engorged crown of his penis with my tongue, teasing him. It was good. Careful, careful—he could go off any minute. I had a sudden urge to do it, to bring him off. To suck hard and feel him throb in my mouth, then lewdly swallow all he gave. But the itch between my legs wanted more. I needed to be fucked.

But first… I sucked him, my throat filled with a man for the first time in what felt like years. I gloried in it, my breasts bared and my panties pulled down, pussy wet and pouting for the cock I now tongued. I licked and sucked him until Brent's fingers tightened in my hair and he sounded as if he were about to erupt. "Ah!" he cried out above me, his prick thick in my throat, my right thumb gentle on his warm, heavy balls. They had drawn up, tightening as I sucked. His cock was getting bigger, swelling. He was close. I swayed on my knees, half-stripped, a lewd vision. My left hand cupped one heavy breast before tangling in my pubic hair, then returning to my tits. Brent wasn't the only one close to orgasm. His cock was yearning in my mouth as my tongue slid along the underside, making him quiver. It was perfect debauchery. I slid one finger inside myself, slippery when wet, oh yes. I was ready. I squeezed him with my right hand, sucked hard, and slowly eased my mouth down his cock until I only had the glans captured. I licked it one last time. "Fuck me," I demanded. I sank down, resting on my thighs, my legs spread open. The invitation was clear. Hell, I probably dripped it on the floor.

Now Brent was down there with me, kissing me, his hands warm on my bare ass. I rose to meet him. His cock poked my belly, and then nudged lower. I twisted up to find it, but was constricted by my jeans. I collapsed, saw the ceiling in a blur, and then he was over me, yanking my jeans down, frantic, his knee working to open my legs. Denim trapped. He kissed me again, his tongue thrusting hot and hard like I wanted his penis to. We wrestled a bit, getting closer and closer, and I felt the blunt head of his cock nudging me, but it was only a tease. His knees weren't up to the oak floor that I loved, and neither was my ass. The surface was cool and unforgiving, and we weren't getting anywhere.

"Over there," I gasped, wriggling in the direction of the foyer, where the kitchen became a wide hall and the carpeting began.

I crawled on my hands and knees, and I didn't have time to feel stupid, for Brent was scrabbling with me, then reaching for my breasts. I knelt, and from behind me he cupped them, gently twisting my nipples. Underneath the imperious ticking of my grandfather clock, he got my jeans off, and I bucked against his hand as it explored me once more. Fingers in my curls, then fingers in my hot, slippery folds. I turned to face him, clutching him, swimming in fire. Then I reached down and clasped him. He was beautiful, the right thing to hold. He fit my hand like a tool crafted just for me. I marveled at how warm his skin was, silky and hard.

I pulled Brent's jeans down, and he got loose. We didn't say a word. I went down on my back, and the carpeting was a better surface for our urgent pairing. Cupping his luscious little ass, tight and firm, I kissed him as his cock prodded my thigh. He still wore his shirt, his belly flat and hard beneath the hem, his cock rearing up dangerously below. I was underneath him, opening my legs without restraint now, and then Brent was over me in the ancient position. So close.

He shifted, kneeling over me. *Don't change your mind now!* I lifted my hips, found his prick, rubbed against it. His face tightened. I couldn't tell if it was desire or torment. "God—I haven't done…" he gasped.

"Don't tell me you're a virgin," I said, as his hands cupped both my breasts. He *couldn't* be a virgin. His mouth traced the slope of my breast as I trapped the head of his penis and began to work it into me. It was driving me crazy—I was so close to what I wanted. Needed. Brent didn't kiss, or move, like a virgin. Just like a young man who'd been without it for far too long. He urgently sought my nipple, risen high and dark pink with excitement. He sucked for a long moment, before he spoke, voice husky. "No, ma'am. I just haven't—I mean, not much. Too busy…"

Too busy? Good grief, he had more discipline than I'd ever had when I was twenty-two. But then, hadn't his ex-girlfriend been much like him? Quiet, religious, a good student? Everything my son wasn't, kids I hoped would be good influences. And here I was, seducing Brent. Some mother I was. I was about to… I didn't want to think. I wanted to fuck. "Please!" I cried, and he shoved hard and entered me. Despite the wetness, I was newly tight. It had been so long that I'd forgotten what it really felt like to open my legs and let a man inside me, to trust that it would give me pleasure.

It was both familiar and strange to feel it about to begin. I drew my knees up and changed the angle, and then he was sliding all the way into me with slow, exquisite friction. It almost hurt, but it felt so good.

Tentative at first, then his strokes quickened, his face a stranger's. He seized my arms and pumped savagely. He kissed me, his mouth impatient, then broke off. I met each thrust, close to climax. Each stroke got me a rung higher up the ladder. The ladder stretched to the sky, to infinity, and I wanted to go all the way up. "Fuck me!" I begged him, clutching his shoulders, twisting the fabric of his shirt. I was soaring and sinning, and he was the only thing that kept me from flying into a million pieces.

Brent pounded into me, making me gasp, and if I was getting rug burns on my ass, I didn't care. No give of mattress made the penetration seem even more powerful, or maybe it was just his youth and my desperation. I wrapped my legs around his slim hips, and lifted my pelvis to meet his thrusts. I was there, tantalizingly close, on the verge of orgasm. This was the moment to hold. If I could have stayed like that forever, I'd offer my mortal soul with no regrets. And then I was coming, hard, rolling into the fire. Release made me cry out, the cold house no longer empty but full of my pleasure.

Too soon it was over, the tide rolling out, Brent still fucking me. I lay there, beneath him, gasping, heart beating a drumbeat to his thrusts. He made a noise to rival mine as he came, going stiff, trapped between my thighs, the sweetest prison a man can find. I watched him come, enjoying the pleasure twisting his face, and saw the man he was, not the boy he'd been. The man in that most private of moments. His climax was like him: strong, intense, somehow pure. Then it was over. He slowed, stopped, throbbing inside me.

"Oh, God," I said, as he panted above me, the only sound our breathing, the only result of pleasure my horror and the beat of my heart, unaccustomed to what we'd done. What we'd done… What *had* I done? Was it worth it?

His eyes were closed, and he looked—happy. Drained. Blissful. Like I felt.

So, hell, yeah—it was worth it. Like Scarlet, I'd let tomorrow take care of itself. Life is short. Winter's cold. Pleasure is rare enough.

THOMAS S. ROCHE

WHILE SHE WAS DANCING

COME ON, I WON'T TELL HER IF YOU DON'T.

It's not as if we *meant* for it to happen. Well…at least *you* didn't. I guess I did, sort of. Anyway, I let it happen. I didn't plan it or anything, but…I knew what was happening, while it was happening—and I let it happen anyway.

So I'll admit it. I'm the bad one. You were just disoriented. I don't know, maybe you were a little drunk, too. And horny. Really, really horny. And hard. Really, really hard. So hard I'm not one hundred percent sure I'm even going to be able to walk today. Which is kind of a good thing…

I won't tell her. You won't tell her. So she'll never, ever know. It'll be our little secret. One I'll never, ever tell *anyone*. But I'll remember it. I'll think about it. Look, I'm not going to lie to you. I'm going to think about it a lot. A whole lot.

A whole, whole lot.

I was turned on, see? Whenever she goes away, I get really turned on. I get wet, like, immediately, before she even closes the door. I know I'm going to have the dorm room all to myself, with plenty of privacy to do…well, things. I have some lingerie, just a little, and I keep it hidden under my mattress. It gets kind of wrinkled, so I have to smooth it out. But it still looks good when it goes on me. It's not much—just a little tiny thong and a camisole that only comes halfway down my stomach, revealing my belly. It looks really good on my breasts; it makes the nipples stand out, peaked, and they're always hard when I'm looking at myself in that outfit.

That's how it started, anyway. I'm not like she is; I don't have the guts to go into Kitten's Top Drawer or wherever and buy any of their really sexy lingerie. But I've seen hers, and she's been in those stores, I can tell. I've seen her underwear drawer. You know, the weekends when she wasn't there. The weekends I was alone.

She's got some awesome sexy lingerie.

So that's what happened last night.

You don't know this, but she left for the weekend. You know that friend of hers from the city? The one who's all hooked in with these famous DJs from Europe and stuff? At the last minute she got passes to this really exclusive club where some really hot DJ was playing. You know how much she likes dancing, right? Yeah, of course you do. She loves to dance. She looks really sexy dancing. Anyway, she got these passes to this special club. She's going to be gone all weekend, and that's why she wasn't here last night. She had to go right away to make it on time, and her cell phone was out of juice, so she couldn't call you. She asked me to tell you. Whoops. Guess I forgot.

I'd tried on a couple of her things before, you know, without asking. She would have loaned me almost anything, but the stuff she kept in her bottom drawer would probably have been going too far. So I didn't ask. I just slipped it out of there and I put it on—the whole outfit, as if I was getting dressed to go out somewhere slutty, like a strip club or something. You couldn't see it last night because it was dark, but I'm sure you've seen it on her before, sometime in good light. The whole outfit is pink and white, kind of virginal but really sexy because it's so skimpy, so lacy, so see-through. I had never seen her in it, but I could imagine, and I bet it looks incredible on her.

I put on a bunch of makeup, that bright red lipstick of hers that she says is called "cocksucker red." She says you always want head when she wears that color. Probably because she tells you it's called that. I put on eye shadow, too, that cheesy '80s blue eye-shadow she wears when she's going out dancing. I looked myself over in the full-length mirror on the back of the door. God, I looked like a tart. The bra is a push-up; she's a little less busty than me so the bra squeezed tight and made my tits look two sizes bigger than they are. They looked all perky and inviting, the way the padding held them.

Then there was her sexy pink garter belt, white stockings, and matching pink and white G-string with an embroidered rose at the top. The G-string part is so, so skimpy. I can't believe she would ever wear it out. The little *V* that dips down where the rose is sits, like, an inch above my pussy. I put the G-string on over my garters, so I could take it off without taking the garter belt off. But then, you already know that part.

See, I guess I had kind of planned it, because I'd seen this outfit in her underwear drawer before. Maybe that's why I shaved when I took a shower yesterday morning. I mean, shaved all the way—even my pussy was smooth. So maybe I *did kind* of plan to try it on. All day yesterday I liked the way it felt, rubbing bare against my tight jeans because I hadn't worn anything under them. I would just die if anyone knew I'd shaved down there.

But now you know, I guess. You found out last night.

It's not like I've got a boyfriend. So there's no one to see it; it's just for my pleasure. I like it smooth down there…but now you know. Now you know everything. You know I shave my pussy and you know what I feel like inside. God, I'm getting wet just remembering.

It was early, like eleven. I ran my hands all over my body, touching the smooth satin and the lace where it caressed my breasts, my belly, my hips, my pussy. There was music outside, a big loud party, everyone getting really drunk. I didn't want to join the party, though. I was having too much fun by myself.

So I turned on music, loud, really loud—like they'd play in a club. You know that CD she has? *American Music to Strip To* or something? Really hard, grinding stuff with lots of women moaning. Lots of guitar, heavy, heavy drums, thick bass… When she plays that album, I always get turned on, even if she's sitting, like, right there. I always get wet.

So I played it loud. That's when I put on that skirt I was wearing. I've seen her wear it lots of times, and I was always kind of jealous. It comes down so low on her hips you can totally see her thong sticking out of it. It's so short that she flashes everyone if she stands up too fast—I mean, like, full on, not just a little glimpse if she's careless.

But you already knew I tried it on, because you took it off me last night. You slid it off me and fucked me. I guess you're the reason I picked that skirt of hers to try on. Because she told me how all she has to do is put that skirt on, and you fuck her good.

She also told me what you did to her the first time she wore it for you. How she found herself out on the bridge, bent over, in the middle of the night, you pulling the skirt up to her waist and just giving it to her, hard, so hard that she came, like, right away and then came again, not even caring if people could hear her. Yup, she told me. She told me about how you pulled the skirt up so high it ripped and she had to sew it, and how you spanked her and called her "Little Girl" and bit the back of her neck and kept talking dirty and all sorts of nasty things like that. God, I got so incredibly wet when she told me about that. I always thought you were so cute, I guess, so maybe that's why I got really turned on, but I bet she looked really good, too, bent over the railing on the bridge with her ass in the air and her legs spread. She told me how she screamed when she came the second time. And the third. You didn't know about the third time, probably. She was embarrassed, because it was when you were spanking her. She came really hard. I shouldn't have told you that. She was embarrassed to tell you that she came from being spanked, but she did. God, I think about that a lot.

In fact, I come all the time, thinking about how good you fucked her on the bridge. That's why I put that skirt on. That's why I put on the little crop top she was wearing that night you fucked her on the bridge, the one you pulled up so you could feel her tits while you gave it to her from behind. The crop top that says PORN STAR, which is kind of what she was that night, since she told me about it and now she stars

— 115 —

in so many of my fantasies, bent over the railing, getting fucked by you while you feel her tits. I love that top on her; it looks great. It totally shows her nipples, because she wears it without a bra. You're probably always looking at her nipples whenever she wears it, I guess. I'm always looking, too. Sometimes it's hard for me to take my eyes off them.

It shows mine, too. My nipples, I mean. Even though I was wearing a bra, it was tight and thin over my nipples, holding my breasts up, pushing them against the tight cotton. Like I said, I'm a little bustier than her, so the crop top was really tight and kind of pulled across my breasts, not really going much below them. I thought the whole thing looked really sexy, especially with the white lace tops of her stockings showing on my thighs, under the hem of the skirt, reminding me how incredibly short the skirt was and reminding me that I was wearing that garter belt. I really looked good. You couldn't see me because it was dark, but I looked really, really good.

I looked especially good as I started dancing for myself, pretending I was a stripper, giving myself a little private dance. I started to get really wet as I saw how good I looked. I ran my hands over my body and pulled up the skirt, showing the G-string and my shaved pussy. I ran my fingertips over the place where the skirt had been mended, remembering how you pulled it up so hard it ripped, how you yanked on it, you were so eager to get your cock inside her. That made me really hot, feeling that rip, actually touching it. I moved with the music, wondering what I would feel like if there was someone there watching me. I looked at my body shimmying and writhing, tried to make my moves sexier, sluttier, more provocative. I looked good. I looked really, really hot.

I looked so hot I kind of lost control.

I got my vibrator out from where I hide it under my mattress and turned around with my back to the mirror, bending over so I could see the skirt riding up on my ass, showing the pink lace panties. I pulled the skirt up and spread my legs a little, watching as I tugged the G-string out of the way.

Then I started fucking myself.

I don't turn the vibrator on when I fuck myself with it, see, I just like the shape. I like the way it's hard against the inside of my pussy, that spot right up from the inside that always makes me come, the G-spot. You know you hit it last night, you hit it perfectly. Something about the way your cock's shaped, I guess. It surprised me, but you hit it dead on, every thrust. God, I'm getting so wet telling you this.

I was bent way over by then and fucking myself from behind, looking over my shoulder so I could watch my ass in the mirror as it swayed back and forth, pretending that I was pushing myself onto a cock instead of pushing a vibrator into me.

I was really close to coming, like, right away. I was so close I had to stop, because I didn't want to come yet. I wanted to dance some more. I moved with the music, feeling it pulse through me. I was so, so wet. I would have fucked just about anyone who walked through that door. No offense.

I started to get all sweaty, dancing in the little room. The crop top started to get a bit soaked. That's why I did what I did next. I went over to her nightstand and got out her perfume. I don't wear perfume, see. And I was…well, to tell the truth I was kind of turned on pretending to be her. She's really sexy, you know? Of course you know. You know exactly how sexy she is.

So I lifted my hair, pointed the mister, and misted.

I think I put on too much. It smelled really strong. But it made me smell like her. I danced some more and got more and more excited. I really wished I had a big mirror by the bed so I could spread my legs and fuck myself in that sexy outfit and watch it as I penetrated my pussy with the vibrator. But I didn't, and if there was one thing I wanted just then, it was to get fucked. So I went over and got onto my bed.

The vibrator went in easy, hard plastic pushing up against my G-spot. I could hear myself moaning, so loud I was afraid I was going to alert the neighbors even over the pounding music. I was going to come any minute, and I wasn't sure I wanted to just yet. I liked fucking myself. I wanted to fuck myself as hard as I could.

Which is how it occurred to me, I guess.

Yeah. She did. She told me everything.

I mean, she gave me the details. Don't worry, I think it's kind of sexy that she likes it that way. Like, brave. Audacious.

I wanted it that way, too. Just like she gets it.

I knew enough to know you had to use something to make it go in easier. Yeah, well, I didn't have any. I mean, when I put that vibrator inside me I never need any kind of lube. I'm always so wet it just goes right in before I even know what's happening. But it's not like I've ever put it in *there*. It's not like I've *ever* put anything in there.

Well, now I have.

But last night, I hadn't.

She has all this lube in her lingerie drawer. I'd seen it when I was looking through her collection. Really big bottles—I mean really, really big, like a pint or something, you know? Of course you know, you do it to her all the time.

I wanted to do it. I mean, I wanted to just try it. I wanted to put something in there, and I was so turned on I knew I could do it.

So I got back on my bed and rolled over on my belly and put my butt in the air and uncapped the lube.

I reached back and poured a little onto my butt…it didn't seem like enough. So I poured a little more, reached back and rubbed it in. I put some on the tip of the vibrator. Kind of a big wet glob. I reached back awkwardly and got ready to push it in.

I got it in, all right—about an inch. It felt good. I mean, really, really good. Yeah, I guess you know that. I guess you know I like it that way. Well, it caught me off guard. My whole body sort of shook and I felt like I was going to come right away.

Which is how it happened—I mean, it was carnage. Total carnage. Lube *everywhere*.

I was totally freaked out—I mean, it was stupid, but I was just so embarrassed. I don't even know where to buy that stuff. I had wasted all her lube and now she was going to find out, plus my bed was now a rapidly growing puddle of goo, right in the middle where I was supposed to sleep. And it's not like my bed is really wide enough for me to sleep over on the side.

I was so mad at myself. I felt really embarrassed. I mean, I figured I was really in trouble.

The towels didn't do anything. Like, anything at all. The lube just kept spreading, soaking through my sheets and making my mattress totally soggy. I knew I should have used a mattress pad. Once I had used every towel in the place to wipe up the lube, my bright idea to sleep on a pile of towels was pretty much not going to happen.

So…well, I mean, it's not like she was going to be using hers, right?

And I was so freaked out, it's not like I was going to get off now. I mean, I would *never* masturbate on her bed. Never.

I was really tired after a full hour of trying to mop up lube from my bed. I was feeling guilty and stupid, and even though my pussy was totally aching, I was too freaked out to try to come anymore.

So I just let it go. But I didn't want to undress. I was exhausted, and besides, I sort of liked having these clothes on.

I was going to have to wash them anyway—so I just stretched, kicked off her high-heeled fuck-me pumps. Took one last look at myself, at how good I looked in the full-length mirror. I blew myself a kiss.

And crawled into her bed.

I love the way she smells. Not just her perfumes and soaps and stuff, but the way her *body* smells. I guess you probably do, too. It's all musky and sexy, and sometimes it just sort of turns me on, smelling her when it's just the two of us or even when she's not here, when I can smell her on her sheets and clothes and stuff.

Okay, I'll admit it. I've smelled her clothes. Not a lot, or anything, but just sometimes when I needed that extra turn-on. She smells really good, doesn't she? Sexy.

So I just curled up there in her bed with the lights out, getting more and more turned on. I really wanted to come. But I felt weird about the lube thing, so I just figured I'd go to sleep.

It took me a long time, like at least an hour, lying there, smelling her, thinking about her, thinking about you. Thinking about the two of you doing it in this bed, where I was trying to sleep. Thinking about you doing...*that* to her.

I touched my pussy a little as I drifted off to sleep. Just to see if I was still wet. I was. Really, really wet. It felt good to touch it, but I knew I shouldn't take it too far. I knew I shouldn't come.

Then I finally managed to get to sleep, and I fell *hard*. You know when you fall really, really deeply asleep all of a sudden? This was like that. When I woke up, I had no idea where I was or what that noise was over by the window.

I saw your leg come in, saw your body follow it. You pulled the window closed and locked it.

It was dark. The lights outside go off at 2:30, you know. I guess it's to save power. So neither of us could see anything.

You're considerate, a gentleman. I heard you tiptoe over to my bed and lean over it. I still didn't remember who I was or where I was or what I was doing there, but thinking back I guess you were checking to make sure I wasn't there.

I heard you pat my pillow, just to make sure. Then I heard your zipper go down. You took off all your clothes. I started to come to my senses as I listened to you undress.

Then I heard your footsteps, soft now as you tiptoed.

I felt your body, sliding under the covers. Naked.

I'll admit it. The second I felt that touch, I wanted it. I wanted you to fuck me. At first I didn't know who I was, if I was her or me, if I was in her bed or mine—if you were her boyfriend or mine. Then, when I felt your body naked against mine, I didn't care.

I was on my back, and I felt your weight on top of me. You're a big guy, and you felt heavy—sexy, hard, imposing. My pussy would have been wet instantly, even if it wasn't before.

You put your face against my neck and took a big, deep breath of me, smelling her perfume. Maybe smelling her scent from her pillow, from her sheets and blankets. I don't know. Whatever it was, you didn't hesitate. You kissed me.

I felt your tongue going into my mouth, teasing me open. I felt my nipples stiffen instantly. I felt my pussy go wet and throbbing, throbbing so hard that I would have done anything, pretended to be *anybody*, to get a cock inside it. And I could feel your cock against me, hard already, pressing on my belly as you kissed me.

I whimpered softly, feeling my nipples harden fully against your naked chest. You knew exactly what I was wearing, knew exactly how to take it off me.

You lifted the crop top and pulled down the bra.

You started suckling on my nipples.

One word. I could have said one word and it would have been all over, you would have known I wasn't her. But I didn't. I bit my lip, didn't even let myself moan for fear you'd recognize that, too. Not that you've ever heard me moan…well, now you have. Now you've heard me moan a lot.

So I just held totally still, felt the electric touch of your lips and tongue on my nipples. Felt your teeth close gently around them, biting me a little.

She likes that, I know. She told me she likes it a lot. Sometimes it can almost make her come. I like it, too, but I've never told anyone that before. I didn't even tell her that when she told me *she* likes it. I just blushed and looked away. I think she likes telling me things that make me blush.

My arms went around your shoulders, and I cradled your head against me. You sucked harder, using your hand to gently pinch and knead my other nipple, while your free hand went down my body.

You felt the skirt and said softly, "Fuck, I love it when you wear this skirt."

You kissed me, then, hard, your tongue going deep inside me. Your cock was really hard against my stomach. It felt really big, a little scary. As you kissed me, I felt you pulling up my skirt.

You took hold of the G-string and pulled it down.

I was immobile, paralyzed, as you slipped the G-string down my stockinged thighs and over my ankles. I couldn't see, but I heard you take a deep breath.

"God, I love the way your pussy smells," you said.

That's when I started moaning. I couldn't stop myself. You were kissing your way back up my body, up my stockings and then around the lace tops, savoring them.

Then you went to work on my thighs.

Your tongue traced circles closer and closer to my pussy.

That's when I passed the point of no return. I really should have said something. I don't know what. Maybe, um, "Don't go down on me, I'm not your girlfriend…"

But I didn't.

Instead, I slowly spread my legs as far as they would go.

The first touch of your tongue on my clit made my whole body convulse, my mouth go wide open, made me claw at the sheets that smelled like her. I stuffed my hand into my mouth and bit down to keep from screaming, it felt so good. It was like I had the vibrator on my clit, like I had it inside me a moment ago, like I was tottering on the brink of orgasm and you came in to push me over the edge.

"You shaved," you said from between my legs, your voice dark and husky with want. "You know I've been wanting that. God, your pussy is so sexy shaved."

Your tongue descended on my clit again and a pathetic little whimper came out of my stuffed-full mouth, my body twisting and writhing on you.

When you pulled up, you said, "I'm going to fuck you so fucking good tonight. I'm going to show you how much I appreciate your doing this for me. Getting all shaved and dressed up for me. You are such a fucking slut and I fucking love it, baby. God, I'm going to fuck you until you scream. You're not going to be able to walk for days, baby."

That's all it took. Just hearing that from your lips was enough to drive me over the edge, but it took the next firm touch of your tongue to really do it. I came so hard, my hand coming away from my mouth and great shuddering sobs of pleasure coming out of my wide-open mouth. I think I came harder than I'd ever come before…though, I'll admit it, not since.

You didn't stop, either. You kept eating me hungrily, like you were desperate for the taste of my pussy, desperate for the feel of its shaved smoothness against your face. I totally lost control. I writhed on the bed and grabbed the pillows and punched them as hard as I could, as

I came and came and came, and you didn't stop until I was whimpering "Please…please…please…" in a little tiny voice, not even able to beg you to stop the pleasure because it overwhelmed me so much. I was totally under your control, helpless on your mouth as you devoured me. I didn't even worry that you'd know who I am, and I guess my voice sounded enough like hers that you didn't realize it. That's when your mouth came away from my pussy and I heard you shifting on the bed, felt the weight of you on top of me.

And I realized it was going to happen.

You were going to fuck me.

I guess I could have stopped then, but there was nothing left of my mind, really. I was just this twisting mass of lust, under you on the bed, wanting your cock so bad I would have told you I was Eleanor Roosevelt if it would have gotten you to put that cock inside me.

I've had sex before. It's not like I'm a virgin. But I don't know if you know this, but you're really, really big. You have a huge, huge cock. Especially the head. It's so thick that if I had had time to think about it I never would have let you put it inside me. I mean, even if you weren't her boyfriend. I already knew you were huge, I mean, she told me— she tells me everything—she told me how she had to get used to it, how she had to try really hard to take it at first. But now she loves it.

I loved it right away, even though I felt that first wave of fear when I realized it was going to happen, when I felt the push of your head against my pussy, felt it sliding up and down between my swollen lips, felt it thick against my entrance. You're used to fucking her, though, and I know she likes it fast and hard—not too much foreplay, not too much teasing, just right in, deep, all the way.

That's how you gave it to me.

But I guess I'm smaller than her, you know, down there. Your head pushed into me and my back arched and, don't get me wrong, it felt so good, so incredible, but I thought at first it was going to rip me in two. I would have stopped you if I could have.

But I couldn't. Because I was still coming.

I mean, not really coming, right in the middle of it. But there were still these spasms going through my body, and it felt like I was going to come again. My pussy was so sensitive, so incredibly sensitive, and clenching so tight from such an intense climax, that it didn't want to accept you.

Besides, it's not like I have a boyfriend. It's not like I'm used to it, really. The last time I had sex was a year ago, and I guess I never really did it all that much anyway. Certainly not with a guy as big as you.

So when the head of your cock popped into me, my mouth went open wide and I reached down, instinctively, my palms spreading against your chest. Not that I wanted you to go out, but my instinct, my reflex, was that I couldn't take it, there was no way I could take it, and so I started to push you away.

I guess she likes it kind of rough. I mean, I knew that. I know about the handcuffs and everything, and how she really likes you to hold her wrists. But it still caught me off guard, totally.

You grabbed my wrists and shoved them down on the bed, leaning forward, your weight holding me down, bearing me into the bed. Then you shoved your cock into me, hard, so fucking hard I thought I was going to explode. I thought I was so stuffed full of your cock that the top of my head would pop off. And you didn't stop there, either.

I guess you like that, too. Like it kind of rough. Like holding her down a little. I mean, nothing too kinky, but I know you do it that way a lot. I know you hold her down and fuck her really hard. Really, really hard.

That's what you did to me, while I was under you, spread and helpless, held down by your weight and your hands on my wrists, forcing them against the mattress, forcing me to take you. I knew that if I opened my mouth, if I spoke one word, the truth would be out. And imagine how it felt when I remembered about that seminar you went to. About the safewords and stuff. And I realized I didn't know her safeword, that nothing I could say would stop you, that I was totally, utterly out of control and, for all intents and purposes, I was yours.

And that's what's really surprising.

Because that's when I came.

Hard. I don't just mean like a continuation of the orgasm I had before, you know, which happens when I'm masturbating sometimes with the vibrator. I mean like a whole new orgasm, on a whole new level. I came so hard as you pounded your cock into me that I swear I must have passed out for a moment. I was just lost in the sensations of your cock violating me, in the feeling of you holding me down on the bed.

I mean, she explained it to me, explained everything. You can always say "safeword," right? So why didn't I say it? Or, I mean, I could have just said your name, you would have recognized my voice, known I wasn't her.

But I didn't. I guess because I didn't want to.

As the sensations began to fade, as the most intense orgasm of my life echoed through my lingerie-clad body underneath your rutting, naked one, I heard you say it. "You're so incredibly tight tonight," I heard you growling roughly, insensitive, callous. "Are you a fucking virgin?"

Which would have upset me sooooooo much at any other time, because I hate it when people think I'm this naïve virgin. But for some reason, that's not how I reacted when you were holding me down and fucking me, telling me how tight my pussy was and asking me if I was a virgin. That's not how I reacted at all.

Instead, I came again.

I'd never had that experience. I mean, to just come like that, randomly, suddenly, not expecting it—it was wild. Totally wild. I would have done anything for you. So when you pulled out of me and grabbed my wrists and forced me up, into a sitting position, it's not like I was going to say "no"—the real "no" *or* the fake "no." I just wanted it, bad, and I knew what was coming.

Okay, I've never done it. I mean, now I have. But I'd never done it before last night. I didn't think I wanted to. And I mean, I *really* never thought I'd do it right after it pulled out of my pussy.

But I was yours. Totally, utterly. Without a will of my own except to get more of your cock—every way I could.

You said, "Suck it!" with this sound that told me you said it to her all the time. I mean, I know she does it. A lot. She really loves it. She talks to me about it all the time. She even loves to swallow.

But it's not that I was afraid you would figure out I wasn't her. I was just…well, I wanted it. I wanted it bad.

So I just sort of *went* with it.

Your cock's really big. Really big. It doesn't even quite fit in my mouth. I have to open wide for it, really wide. But I did open wide, and I just sort of started *sucking* it.

God, it was incredible. I could feel my pussy throb with each stroke I gave you down your thick shaft. I wanted it so bad, I wanted all of it.

I know she deep-throats. I mean, she tells me everything. She even told me how to do it. I don't think she ever thought I'd be doing it to *you*, though.

But at that moment, I didn't care. I just wanted it in me, all the way.

So I took a deep breath. A really, really deep breath, because your cock's really big. And as I felt the head, thick against the back of my throat, I swallowed.

Don't get me wrong, I was scared. You're huge. And I'd never done it before. Never sucked cock, I mean. And definitely never had anything down my throat. I mean, I was *beyond* scared. I just wanted it really, really bad. If I could have backed out, I would. But it's not that you wouldn't let me back out—all I had to do was say your name and you'd know who I was. It was that I couldn't bear the thought of not having your cock every possible place in my body that it would fit—even if it didn't, you know, really fit.

I counted. It took me, like, eight tries. I know it sometimes takes her two or three, so I felt my face reddening and I was afraid you'd know I wasn't her because it took me so long to get it down. But if you noticed the difference, you didn't say anything. Instead, you just put your head back and moaned.

God, it was a turn-on. Hearing you moan like that, and knowing I was doing it to you. If I'd had my vibrator on my clit, I would have come. But of course, that was out of the question—she hates vibrators. Never uses them.

So I just reached down and touched my clit, and it happened again.

It was getting strange. I mean, I'd never come like that before, and I didn't even think girls *could* come from giving head. I mean, you know, that movie *Deep Throat* isn't real, is it? I don't fucking know, but the fullness of your cock down my throat just made me do it. It felt like there was a direct connection between your cock and my clit, and I only had to rub myself, like, three little, little strokes to make it happen.

Your hips pumped rhythmically and my face met each thrust. Now it was easy; my throat felt wide open and I was totally into the rhythm of it. I didn't even think about how big your cock was in terms of not being able to take it. I thought about how turned on I was to be swallowing it, wanting it, needing it more than I'd ever needed anything. I could hear you moaning in that way guys do, you know, not that I have a lot of experience, but I've heard it before, and I know what it means. You were close. Really, really close. And I knew that maybe if I kept doing what I was doing you'd come, just come right in my mouth. Down my throat. That sent a fresh, intense, overwhelming surge of excitement through my body, and I wanted it. I wanted your come, even though I'd never tasted it before, even though I had no idea if I'd even be *able* to swallow. But I know she swallows, so I figured it'd be okay. And I wanted it so bad, I would have done anything to get it.

But you had other things in mind. You weren't finished with me yet.

You guided me onto my hands and knees. I know she loves it this way. I like it too. I mean, I haven't done it that much, but I knew I liked it. I fantasize about it a lot.

Your cock still seemed huge, though. It was harder for me to take it in this position. My pussy felt tighter, and your cock felt bigger. Maybe that's why I gasped, why I moaned so loud when I felt your cockhead against my pussy again.

But I wanted it. I really, really wanted it.

So I pushed back onto you, and you gave it to me, fast, like I know she likes it. Like *I* like it, I guess. Like I wanted it, then, hard, merciless, driving into me so it almost hurt—almost, but not quite.

And you fucked me. You fucked me hard, fast, your hips pumping your cock into me as I fucked back onto you. God, I came so hard. I don't know how, I shouldn't have been coming. I mean, I'd already come three times…four? Maybe five. I don't know. But I came again. I came so hard and I just moaned and moaned, not even caring whether you realized it was me. Not caring about anything but your cock, deep inside me, hitting my G-spot like I told you. Maybe that's why I came so hard. Maybe that's why I wanted you to come inside me so bad.

But you didn't. Not there, anyway. I felt your hand tracing a path down my back, over the bunched-up skirt, over the garter belt. I felt your thumb press against my hole.

I heard you chuckling, knowingly.

"You're ready for me," you said.

Your cock felt as big coming out as going in. It left this big void inside me, inside my pussy, a void I wanted filled.

"Please," I moaned softly. "Please…please…"

I guess I knew it was coming. I guess I wanted it. Yes, I definitely wanted it. I was a little scared—I mean, it had felt so good when I put that vibrator in my butt, just a little way, but your cock is so, so big. I mean, really big.

But I didn't tell you to stop. I couldn't even summon a request for you to slow down. I know it was hard for her at first to take it that way, because you're so big. But now she takes it easily, and she likes it that way. And you love to give it to her.

So you didn't slow down. You didn't give it to me gently.

You pushed into me, and my eyes went wide in the darkness. Sensation flooded my body. My pulse pounded in my ears, and I felt my hole expanding—I thought it was going to hurt, and maybe it did, a little, just for a second. But then you were in me, and I couldn't believe it, but I was opening up for it. I was taking it that way—the way I thought I couldn't. The way *she* likes it, you know—the dirty way, I guess.

And God, it felt so incredible.

It felt so good that I pushed back onto you. I felt you going deep into my ass, and you didn't give me a moment to catch my breath.

You started fucking me fast, hard, like you didn't care if it felt good. But it did. It felt incredible. Remember what I told you about your cock and my G-spot? I know it's not possible, but it felt like your cock was hitting right there—almost like it was hitting my clit from the *inside*. I knew I was going to come.

And you were, too. I'm really tight back there, I guess, and maybe it just felt really good to you. But you weren't in there very long, maybe twenty strokes, thirty, I don't know. I heard you groaning and I knew you were going to come in my ass.

Which drove me right over the edge, into the most intense orgasm of them all. I came so hard I think I bit my lip. It still feels raw. I think I actually started crying, it felt so good. I grabbed at the pillows and threw them across the room. I pushed my hands against the wall and shoved myself onto you. I felt you pumping and heard your moans and knew you were coming inside me, somewhere no come had ever been.

It seemed like you came for a really long time. When your cock slid out, my legs were weak and I was shaking. You slumped down on the bed next to me and I writhed there, not believing the sensations that were going through my body.

It was like I was in a trance. I stripped off my clothes, wriggling around on the bed, just because I wanted to feel my naked body against yours. You stayed still, breathing heavily, while I rubbed my body all over you. You were moist with sweat. I licked it off your chest and the salty taste made me so hungry for you I could feel my pussy hurting, wanting your cock, still, despite how good you'd given it to me. I felt really sad, like I wished I could have it every night for the rest of my life, have your cock inside me. But I knew I couldn't, so I decided to just love you while I could. What the hell, right? It's not like you were complaining.

I snuggled up against you, feeling your naked body against mine and I listened to you sleep.

So that's what I remember. But one thing I know—we should never, ever do it again. Never.

I didn't sleep at all, just sprawled there with my face against your chest, smelling you, not even able to smell her anymore. I just felt your chest rise and fall as you slept, felt the softness of your cock, slick and savory in my hand as I cradled it, remembering what it felt like inside me. I felt my heart pound, and thought and thought and thought about what I was going to say when you woke up.

And so I guess this is what I said, to tell you the story and let you know why it happened. To answer the question on your face when you looked into my eyes, to answer the many questions, and maybe hope that you would tell me your side of it, so I would understand why in all those questions I saw in your eyes there wasn't the faintest hint of anger, or regret, or even, I guess, really, guilt.

I still don't know why you looked at me so naturally, why you looked at me and smiled—surprised, sure. But pleased, maybe; satisfied, even? I don't know—relieved? It was kind of weird. You looked like you were glad to see me. And instead of saying, "What the fuck are you doing here with my come in your ass?" you just smiled, stroked my hair, and said my name. You've got to admit that was pretty weird.

It was an accident. And we should never, ever do it again.

What are you doing? Oh, wow. You shouldn't. Yes, that feels good, sure, but...no. Don't do that. No, really. I'm serious. *Safeword safeword safeword.*

Oh, wow.

ALISON TYLER

ON FINDING JON'S PORN

"COMPUTERS SUCK!"

I said the words in my head, and then out loud, but the statement didn't make me feel any better. I was working late on a homework assignment. The simplest kind, and therefore the easiest to forget. My computer died midway through on the night before my deadline. The globe with a tiny question mark inside turned around and around. Rebooting only seemed to make the machine madder. I know I could have gone to the student center and rented time on a computer there, but I was lazy. Instead, I sat on the edge of my twin bed in a sulk, kicking the metal bed frame like a four-year-old who didn't want to take a nap. Over and over my bare heel connected with the metal, creating a satisfying thud each time. I might have spent the entire night like that, if Jon hadn't stopped by and taken the time to ask me what was wrong.

"Deadline," I told him, "and dead computer." I gestured hopelessly to the ever-spinning globe on my screen. Round and round and round it went. Mesmerizing. Dizzying.

"Take my laptop," Jon offered immediately. "No problem. I'll print your paper for you when you're finished."

I gazed up at him, realizing that this meant I actually had to get back to work. "You're a lifesaver," I told him, only half-kidding.

"You haven't heard what my payment is going to be," he said, grinning at me.

I typed in the first half of the paper from scratch, and then, feeling as if I'd been wasting my time doing the same thing twice, I started to poke around on his computer. As I said, I was lazy. Besides, Jon's files seemed way more interesting than my paper on the floor patterns of Prussian churches.

On finding Jon's porn, I knew that my evening was going to end decidedly differently than it had started. On finding Jon's porn, I knew that Jon was an entirely different person than I had thought he was when we started.

He looked like a choirboy. White-blond hair, pale blue eyes, a Brooks Brothers sense of style in an Urban Outfitters world. His dorm room was always clean and neat, to the point of being obsessively so. I didn't know anyone else who sent their shirts out for laundry, not any junior in college, anyway, nor any other student who owned his own vacuum. He was a Third—as in, Jonathan Elliot Dawson the Third—and he had an unshakable vision of his future. One that he would share with his closest friends. One that involved a top-floor office, a forty-foot yacht, a vacation home on Arrowhead Lake.

But what I now discovered, to my great shock and darkly twisted satisfaction, was that he also had a massive, overpowering, intoxicating collection of raw, stark porn downloaded from the Internet. My eyes scanned picture after picture, rabidly, hungrily. I felt myself growing ever more aroused, and I started clicking with only one hand, so that I could cradle my pussy with the other, pressing two fingers directly against my clit through my faded old jeans.

Unlike Jon's other female friends, the ones who lived in sorority houses and wore matching pastel sweater sets, I was far more Aardvark's Odd Ark than Ann Taylor. I possessed a vintage aesthetic that led me to wear perhaps a bit more black than I should have. My glasses sported rhinestones on their catlike corners. My shoe collection included a range from spectators to bowling. An odder couple you wouldn't easily find—but in fact Jon and I were tight friends. The type to stay up late over coffee and discuss our future. The type to lend a computer to a chum in need.

Might we be more than friends? I'd never considered the possibility before. Had I been lazy in that respect, too?

When Jon stopped by to see how the paper was progressing, I didn't even pretend not to have found his stash. I glanced over my shoulder, and then back to the screen, waiting to see what he'd say. What he'd do. Would he flush in embarrassment, mortified by what I had found? Or would he dredge up a quick lie, claiming that the pictures were someone else's? That his roommate, Lawrence, had borrowed his PowerBook and had taken the time to download the thousands of pictures I'd had the luck to discover. Or would he become self-righteous? What in the hell was *I* doing looking through his personal belongings, rifling through file after file, my sticky fingerprints all over the keyboard? Hot and wet.

He did none of those things. Instead, he came to stand behind my desk chair and set his large, strong hands on my shoulders and leaned forward, looking at the pictures with me. I could feel his body behind mine, and I paid attention to him in a way I never had before.

"That—" he said, tapping the screen lightly with one finger. "That one's my favorite."

I could have guessed.

All were photos of a certain type, specifically anal, and this particular picture showed a man parting a girl's rear cheeks and lubing her up with a torrent of clear K-Y. You could see her puckered asshole, shaved, beautiful. You could see how rock hard he was, and you could just guess what it was going to feel like when he filled her. Or, at least, I could.

"Do you like it, too?" he asked.

I nodded. "Close the door—"

"Your roommate—" he reminded me.

"Out of town—"

"Do you have—"

All our sentences were like this. Disjointed. Rushed. Yet perfectly clear to the two of us, and that's all that mattered.

"Yeah," I told him, squirming out from between the chair and the desk to pull open the drawer at the side of my tiny twin bed. He wanted lube. I had lube. He wanted more than that—I was stripping before he could even tell me what to do. It was obvious, wasn't it? He wanted me naked, spread out on my bed, my ass toward him. And I wanted that, too.

I watched over my shoulder as Jon undressed. He took off his clothes far more slowly than I had, surveying the scene in front of him with a look of total contentment on his face. Complete control. Next to me was the computer, with the image of the lovely young model showing off her perfect asshole. And on the left was me, doing the same exact thing, as if Jon had downloaded me from the website.

"God, you're beautiful," he said, his breath against my spine. "I've been fantasizing about this for months—"

And then his mouth was lower, moving swiftly to kiss between my rear cheeks, licking and tickling me as he readied me for step two. But he didn't hurry the foreplay. I wouldn't have thought he would. Not after looking at all those pictures. He seemed like someone who definitely wanted to build up to the climax. How he built managed to surprise me even more.

"You didn't finish your paper, did you?" he whispered, his mouth against me.

I shook my head.

"You decided to be a little snoop instead." In between his words, his tongue worked magic over me. He traced it up and down between the crack of my ass, and then he plunged forward. I don't think I'd ever been that turned on before. I was already dripping wet from my foray through his gallery of porn. Now, with his mouth on me, I knew I was only seconds from coming.

"A snoop who could use a little discipline—" he hissed, and I shuddered all over. Something seemed to snap in me as Jon pushed me down on the bed and held me pinned there, like a butterfly, beating uselessly to get free. He used his bare hand on my ass, smacking my right cheek and then my left, repeatedly punishing me while he spoke. I stared at the girl on the screen. She could use a spanking, too, couldn't she? I glanced over my shoulder at Jon, my eyes moist, my pussy far wetter. How had he known? How could he tell?

The sounds of our dorm mates echoed down the halls. Were they having yet another shaving cream fight? How totally juvenile. Jon and I were the adults. Or, rather, he was, spanking my tail until I started to moan, and then returning to his previous mission, spreading apart my asscheeks and sliding his cock into my rear hole.

While I looked at the picture on his screen, he rode me, as hard as I'd ever been taken. He fucked me like all the lovely girls on the computer were getting fucked. And I came like them—powerfully, uncontrollably. Shocked at myself. And shocked at Jon.

You see, on finding Jon's porn, I realized that I was definitely going to miss my deadline—but I wasn't concerned about that any longer.

Sometimes deadlines are worth missing. Sometimes secrets are worth sharing. Jon's collection was just such a secret—one we kept between us for the rest of the year.

ABOUT THE EDITOR

CALLED "A TROLLOP WITH A LAPTOP" by *East Bay Express*, Alison Tyler is naughty and she knows it. Ms. Tyler is the author of more than twenty explicit novels, including *Learning to Love It*, *Strictly Confidential*, *Sweet Thing*, *Sticky Fingers*, and *Something About Workmen* (all published by Black Lace), as well as *Rumors*, *Tiffany Twisted*, and *With or Without You* (Cheek). Her novels and short stories have been translated into Japanese, Dutch, German, Italian, Norwegian, and Spanish.

Ms. Tyler's short stories in multiple genres have appeared in many anthologies as well as in *Playgirl* magazine and *Penthouse Variations*.

She is the editor of *Batteries Not Included* (Diva); *Heat Wave, Best Bondage Erotica* volumes 1 & 2, *The Merry XXXmas Book of Erotica*, *Luscious*, *Red Hot Erotica*, *Slave to Love*, *Three-Way*, *Happy Birthday Erotica*, *Caught Looking* (with Rachel Kramer Bussel), and *Got a Minute?* (all from Cleis Press); *Naughty Fairy Tales from A to Z* (Plume); and the *Naughty Stories from A to Z* series, the *Down & Dirty* series, *Naked*

Erotica, and *Juicy Erotica* (all from Pretty Things Press). Please visit www.prettythingspress.com or www.alisontyler.blogspot.com.

Ms. Tyler is loyal to coffee (black), lipstick (red), and tequila (straight). She has tattoos, but no piercings; a wicked tongue, but a quick smile; and bittersweet memories, but no regrets.

In all things important, she remains faithful to her partner of eleven years, but she still can't choose just one perfume.